You Made My Heart a Hunter

E. M. Epps

This is a work of fiction. Any references to real people or places are used fictitiously. Other names, characters, places and events are products of the author's imagination, and any resemblance to actual events or places or persons, living or dead, is entirely coincidental.

Copyright © 2014 E. M. Epps. All rights reserved.

Cover design © 2015 E. M. Epps. Photo of forest © Scott Wylie via Flickr, adapted under the terms of the Creative Commons license. Photo of Zitkala-Sa is public domain. Photo of woman with sword © Can Stock Photo Inc / Goga.

Authors thrive on reviews! Please consider leaving one on your review site(s) of choice.

This story and its title were inspired by the song "Fallen Icons" by Delirium.

You are welcome to pronounce the characters' names however you like. But, for the curious, here are the *very* approximate English pronunciations of some of the less intuitive foreign words appearing in this story (with 'zh' being like 's' in *pleasure*, and 'gh' being a somewhat harsher 'h'):

Aistra Isshainto – *eye* struh ih *shine* toh
Damaiud – dah *my* ood
Davrith – *dahv* reeth
Ereshezhu Farogento – eh reh *sheh* zhoo fah rog *en* toh
Hadhera – hah *there* uh
Hena – *hen* uh (the plural is Heina, *hay* nuh)
Henanue – huh *nah* noo eh
Herede – heh *red* eh
Hoei Madruanto – *ho* ay ma droo *ahn* toh
Kasith – kah *seeth*
Lhennuen Hegaantendre – *len* oo un heh gahn *ten* dreh
Nazu Sasange – *nah* zoo sah *song* eh
Siol – *see* oll
Soskulus – *soh* skoo looss
Tayitoös – ta yee *toh* ohss
Teido Nazunto – *tay* doh nah *zoon* toh
Tsiani – tsee *ah* nee
Yugho – *yoo* gho

When the head priestess came to tell Lhennuen that her husband had died, she already knew. In fact, she had known since that night, when she had awakened in the pitch black and had barely made it to the chamber pot before being violently sick.

Since she was a Siol and a priestess of Hadhera, and could be neither pregnant nor ill, the cause had to be outside of herself. A moment's searching through her mind produced the answer.

She wept only very briefly, on the floor beside the chamber pot in the dark. Her husband had told her the first time they had met that he would not live out four years; and she, Seer, had seen the truth of it. Davrith had told her that he would not court her if she did not want to marry a fated man. She had married him anyway.

She had done all of her weeping at the time. There was no need for any more.

Just after dawn, the head priestess knocked on the door to her room. Lhennuen was sitting on the bed with her back to the door, turning over in her hands the painted bone comb her husband had given her as a betrothal present.

"Come in," she said in a low even voice, without turning.

The head priestess put her head around the door with a tentative manner unlike her usual self.

No one knew how old Hapato was. A hundred years was a common guess. So old that her back was stooped, her face a walnut of wrinkles beneath a thin white fluff of hair, her voice trembling—all despite her power as a Siol, which could hold off such things for a long time. But then, most Siols died for their work, and never had the chance to grow old.

"Do you know?" Hapato asked.

"I know," Lhennuen said calmly.

"I share your grief," said Hapato, speaking the truth rather than just the traditional condolence.

Lhennuen looked around at her mistress—her friend. Lhennuen's face, narrow, dark-eyed, composed, and very white, was a pale blot in the dim room lit only by the soggy light entering through the window. Lhennuen was a young woman, but her eyes were not and never had been the eyes of a youth.

Hapato noticed that she had not covered her hair today as a married woman did.

"Thank you, Hapato," said Lhennuen. "That means much to me." She shifted her position sideways on the edge of the bed to look at Hapato steadily. "Come in," she said a second time.

Hapato entered, and closed the door, but stayed near it.

"How did he die?" Lhennuen asked.

If Hapato was surprised that Lhennuen had not seen that as well as the death itself, she did not betray it. Prophecy and the sight of distant things were fickle gifts.

Hena friends do not spare each other truths. "Disembowelment," said Hapato.

Rather than horror, a small flash of understanding passed across Lhennuen's face. The reason for the stomach cramps, then. Then her face closed, keeping her feelings inside, though her eyes were more shadowed than usual.

"Ah," she said.

Then a moment later, she said: "Is the name of the one who killed him known?"

A pulse jumped in Hapato's throat. Revenge was forbidden by the Hena religion, which was not to say it was not widely practiced.

"It is."

"If it is in your power," Lhennuen said, "will you try to see that my mother does not find it out?"

Hapato relaxed.

"She will not ask," she said, speaking truth, though the elder Damaiud had not yet been informed. If any among them would pursue vengeance over the adopted son of her house, it was she.

Lhennuen smiled faintly. "Good for her," she said. "Personal growth for Hamyenev Damaiud."

It was only because she was a Siol, and Lhennuen Damaiud, did she say such a thing to someone who was not a member of her family.

"How did he die?" she asked again. A different question, this time.

"The post was ambushed at night. He was the one who raised the alarm, saving others. Other than that, I don't know."

Lhennuen nodded, with relief.

"Good," she said in a low voice, as if to herself. "He was always afraid his death would not be useful. He can rest in peace, then."

Then she looked at Hapato. She started to ask something; then stopped herself visibly, and bit her lip.

Hapato guessed. "He was elsewhere, I imagine," she said gently.

There were thousands of miles of border along the river Zhelne, and only three or four hundred Siol—priests and priestesses serving the gods Hadhera, Baros, Seddes, and Ainos—on regular guard rotation. Lhennuen was on that rotation herself, but she was in the middle of her yearly four months' temple duty. Even a Siol must rest.

And even a Siol cannot be in two places at once. Not Lhennuen, and not the one who worked in the area where Davrith had served.

"I've certainly killed enough men on my watch," Lhennuen said in a calm voice, "by not being in the right place at the right time. Don't worry, Hapato, I bear no one a grudge."

"Even the Tsiani?"

Lhennuen's eyes unfocused as she thought about it in silence, testing to see if what she had previously decided was still true.

"They're fools to fight this war," she said at last; "and I don't understand why they do. But then, I'm sure they think we're fools not to go south and kill them all, and end it. No, I don't hate them."

Hapato was silent, not disagreeing.

Lhennuen's eyes grew sharp again. She leaned toward the head priestess, resting one hand on the embroidered bedspread. "Hapato?"

"Yes?"

"I don't feel quite human," Lhennuen said frankly.

Hapato caught the meaning under the words. Not *today*, Lhennuen meant, but *always*. She was astonished, but only for an instant. At the end of the instant, after the history of her experiences with Lhennuen had unraveled back through time and rewritten itself forwards once more with this new knowledge, she realized that the astonishment was not because of the statement but because it had been said aloud.

Hapato, for all her power, had always felt human: had felt as intensely as anyone the pains and joys of the heart, if not the body.

"When I was young," Lhennuen said, "I thought that what was lacking was the fact that I was not a Siol, but was supposed to be. After I became a Siol, I realized that the grey robe gave me permission to act as I felt, and that was a relief, a great comfort. Nevertheless, I understand what it means to be human, and I'm not quite it. Am I." She smiled a little, wryly.

Hapato was almost frightened. She had known Lhennuen ever since the young woman had come at age thirteen, a new-minted Siol, to become a priestess. No, she would never have said that Lhennuen was usual; but what Siol is?

The answer came to her thickened tongue of its own accord, not through any thought of her own.

"That's your power," she said.

Lhennuen looked at her, questioning.

"You told me how you became a Siol," Hapato said, her tongue in her own control again. "You leapt, and flew. Did you ever think that anyone who could fly so easily could ever be entirely human?"

Lhennuen looked amused. "Well...."

"But tell me this. Do you love?" Hapato asked.

"Yes," Lhennuen said.

"And are you ever afraid?"

Lhennuen looked thoughtful, and didn't answer for a moment. "Only in matters of love," she said after a while, "and not for long."

"That's enough," Hapato said.

Lhennuen smiled wryly. "Do you think?"

Hapato at last came and sat beside her on the edge of the bed. "What matters," she said, "is that you find the proper use for that power, which has burned through you for many lifetimes, making you what you are."

Lhennuen was still; then she nodded slowly. Her eyes, clear and dark and without age, held Hapato's gaze. "You're right. Thank you, Hapato." She paused, looking almost ashamed. "I wasn't going to tell you this now, but...I'm leaving."

Hapato was so startled she drew back.

"Leaving the priesthood?"

Lhennuen shook her head. "No. I've no desire to do that. But I am leaving here—leaving the temple, leaving rotation." The shame was gone from her face as she said, "I'm sorry to leave you short. But I have to go. I've known this for a while, halfway, but now with Davrith gone, I can, must, leave."

"Go where? Home?"

"No. I...have to wander. I have to move." She raised her hands and dropped them helplessly, unable to explain with words. Then she said in a clear voice: "I have to discover what use this power is for. Because it's too big for what I'm doing with it."

She did something Hapato had never seen her do; she held up her hands and without any hesitation or effort raised a ball of crackling blue power between them, a barely-contained sphere of light and heat, silver-blue streaks skimming and jumping on its surface as if it might explode at any second. Hapato's eyes were cut sharply after the dull light of the day, and she looked away in shock. No one did magic like this. Magic, to the priests and priestesses of Hadhera, was the magic of war: shields for defense, and silent death (why waste one's time and energy with any other kind?), and little tricks with the wood of wagon wheels to ruin supply lines, and healing when no priest of Isura was near.

It was true that Hapato or any Siol could raise a light. It was true, indeed, that any streetcorner magician could raise a light. But Hapato's senses beyond the power of sight told her that the light in Lhennuen's hands was not just a showman's trick, but the raw power of universes.

The light went out.

"So I have to go," Lhennuen said. There were tears in the corners of her eyes as she looked at Hapato, but they never interfered with her ability to see. "I'll miss you. And the temple, and all of you."

It occurred to Hapato that it was possible to be both human, and not. She reached out to touch her friend and take her hand, because no priestess of Hadhera is a coward, in either matters of war or friendship.

"Where will you begin?" she asked.

"In the woods," Lhennuen said. "That is, after all, where our people were born. Maybe I will be, too."

*

The next day, Lhennuen was in the forest near the northern border.

She had added her grey sorcerer's robe over her lapis Hadhera-blue dress; had strapped her mess kit over it and belted her silversword to her side. Other than that she was as she had been the day before, without hat or coat or heavy boots. It did not matter. She wished to neither freeze nor be soaked with snow melted by her own warmth, so as soon as she realized where her Gate had brought her, she set a spell so she would become neither. The only chill was in the air she breathed, for her magic hadn't time to warm it fully before her lungs needed it.

And her head and her ears felt cold: but that was her imagination. She should still be wearing the headscarf of a married woman until the mourning period had passed; but she had barely been able to bring herself to touch it since it had become a lie yesterday.

For a long moment after closing her Gate, she stood still and looked around. The trees, some dark-needled and some leafless skeletons, thin and heaven-high, were sleeping beneath a thick coating of snow. The sky above them glowed a weak grey from the sun behind a solid sheet of cloud. The silence was absolute.

Lhennuen felt a deep relief. She breathed out in a long sigh. To be alone, right now, was what she needed. The only person she could share aloneness with was Davrith. He'd understood it was possible to touch and love and share a life, and yet, at times, be silent together.

It was in her nature to treat her own mental state with dispassion: she'd always been curious how she would feel when he died. Now she knew. Other than that one moment in the dark, she had not been wracked with grief. She didn't fear it if it came again—but she didn't think it would.

Many would think her cold for that. But they didn't know the half of it. She did, and she did not judge herself.

She and Davrith had met by chance, both far from home, then courted by letter for a half a year. And it was during their courtship that she *had* grieved for him, endlessly, with all the intense passion of a fifteen-year-old; though she had been grateful that he had not been there to see. It did not seem right that he should witness it.

Then when they had married she had let the grief go, taking comfort in the other side of it: that he would not die *before* his time, either. That had helped a surprising amount, when they were stationed in different war zones.

Their marriage never would have worked had she not been a Siol. But she could visit him in one step, and, with the careful arrangement of duty schedules, they had been able to spend most nights together.

Now that what he had foreseen had happened at last, all she

could feel was relief at having it over with, and a hollow in her heart where something had been taken out. The gap didn't bother her unless she prodded it.

But she had discovered that it was the expectations of other people—expecting her to feel something she did not feel, to act in a way she could not act—that she was incapable of handling. In a time of change, she felt the requirements of intimacy like a weight. Of course she had gone to Davrith's funeral that morning, but the only other attendees had been his compatriots on the base where he'd served, and they knew her well enough to not require from her some wild public display of grief...of which the mere thought left her more exhausted than the grief itself.

Yet other than that, seeking out one young fellow priestess-friend to give the news to, giving her horse a kiss, and leaving a note for her family: that had been the extent of her ability to make goodbyes.

Then she'd drawn her sword and used it to cut a Gate in the air. She chose no particular destination, but said: "What You will."

And now she was here.

As soon as she shifted her weight, the crust of snow crunched beneath her. Absently she flicked a spell around her feet, and then stepped lightly, just on the powdery surface. She would barely leave footprints.

For a while she felt the solid warmth of Davrith, just behind her to the right. She did not look around, accepting it and taking comfort from it. Maybe it was her imagination; maybe it was his spirit come to visit her. She preferred not knowing. The presence allowed her to relax, and not think for a while. She walked for—an hour or two? She wasn't sure. What finally disturbed her peace was pangs of hunger. The mental energy required to keep up her spells was still energy, and had to be replenished somehow.

For a fanciful moment she considered changing into a dragon, as she had that first time, when she had leapt from Huolle Gorge into a new life. Dragons, not being real, didn't need to eat. She grinned.

"But the tail and wings would be terribly inconvenient in a forest," she said to her imaginary Davrith, careful to not look to her right as she stopped for a moment to fish into her bag for some bread.

She ate as she walked, a good wheat bread with a crust that crunched. She knew it wouldn't hold her for long, but she was unconcerned. She could hunt, and surely would have to soon if she wanted to stay here. But this was where God wanted her to be; and she would not leave until she had discovered why. She intended to find a good place, and try her skill at building a cabin in which to think for a while.

Besides, she enjoyed hunting. It seemed to be the only time when her powers were so focused she left rational thought behind.

*

When it began to get dark, far sooner than she would have expected, she changed her mind about the pleasures of being alone. The sense of Davrith had long since left and the cold pressed in from every side. She could sense it on the bubble of her spell, even when she could not feel it on her skin. Her heart felt small and cold in her chest as if it had shrunk.

For a while she was able to remind herself that she was a Siol, and a priestess of Hadhera and of the God bigger than She.

No worldly ill could touch her, unless she let it. That thought would bring a flush of warmth for a little while. Then she was having to repeat it to herself every moment, and ceased to believe it.

She stopped in the darkening wood, astonished to discover that she was afraid. She wrapped her arms around herself and looked through trees looming black and uncaring. She knew with her mind that if need be she could wake them up, and they would watch over her. She knew with her mind that she could raise a witchlight, or even see in the dark if she wanted. She knew with her mind that she could draw her sword and Gate to anywhere she wished. Her mind knew these things; it was her heart and body that had failed her. The idea of acting, of moving, of speaking, was beyond her will. The shadows were an inviolate force and to bring light among them was impossible—unthinkable. Her fear was not one of death or hurt or the unknown but fear for fear's sake, the nameless terror of a nightmare, where the world doesn't work as it should, where you speak and make no sound, run and move nowhere, raise a hand and no power comes. She drew her power hard inside her body, keeping it close like the hard shell of a nut to protect herself against unknown enemies. She shivered, trembling with fear. She knew with the small part of her being still capable of knowing that she had to sing, that it would be all right if she sang, but she was frozen, incapable of freeing herself. She hoped for a motion in the woods: something alive, something mundane, a bird or a lynx, that would break this spell she had put on herself. But no rescue came.

She shivered, and did what she could do: she listened.

Outwards, said the voice.

But I'm afraid, she said.

The fear tumbled out of her towards the voice, in a silent plea. Send her magic outwards? She couldn't. It was the only thing protecting her. She hardened it around herself.

It's going to shrink if you hold it close like that; send it outwards! Come what may, you'll be alive tomorrow.

That was the thing she needed to be reminded of. Her paralysis was lessened by a brief flash of confidence.

But it was a bittersweet knowledge. Being reminded of that, that she would have to go on, tomorrow and the day after and the day after, because she was too powerful to be killed and too powerful to have to sacrifice herself: that was part of what frightened her in the first place.

But with her fear named, she could work around it. Shaking and nearly weeping with terror in what was now a nearly pitch-black forest, she used every ounce of strength she had to force herself to lower her arms to her sides, feeling as if she would be stabbed by the dark as soon as she did. Her breath refused to come from her throat. She could not think of a spell, or words to make one, or any appropriate song. She was sobbing.

Davrith, I need your help. Help—

Even if she could have called his ghost from the plane of death in this state of mind, he could not have helped her.

Still sobbing, she threw herself against the fear of her body as if it were a physical thing, and pushed through with a song that was wrong, yet it was the only one she could think of. A song in Hadra, yes, but a folksong, a love song.

"*Keut sem—*" she choked, feeling that ripping the night with words was the blackest sin for which she could never be forgiven. "*Keut sem er ta—*"

Oh let me be—

She was shaking too hard to speak. She forced it out regardless. *"Sudi kei zhavadin."*

—the moon in your night.

"Keut sem er ta utru kei dheirshaudin."

Oh let me be the water in your well.

She began to sing the refrain far too rapidly, because the more of it behind her, the easier the way forwards would be.

I will be anything, for you.

Oh my love, please!

Oh let me be

The grain in your field.

Oh let me be

The hand in your hand.

I will be anything, for you....

With the refrain she realized that the lyrics were right after all, though it was not a lover she was speaking to, but that thing greater than herself which she served. A shaky, ironic smile touched her lips. She was able to breathe again.

Very funny, she thought, as she started to sing it over again, more strongly. She straightened her back, feeling the shudders drip away.

I will be anything, for you.

—and I know you'll tell me what it is you want me to be for You —when you're ready. I do have faith in that.

Forcing through the final dregs of fear, she raised her hands and let her power loose, like a fermented bottle too long stoppered. Blue light scraped the heavens and lit the sky.

Use it how You will, she said.

*

She had sung until her eyes closed and would not open. She slept at the base of a tree and woke with a start to find that it was full light. Birds were singing in a polyphony of trills. Lhennuen stretched her arms stiffly, looking around. Her heart and mind and magic were wrung out, exhausted, but it was a satisfying exhaustion, like one has after art or love. Her limbs were trembling a little, but she decided not to worry about it until she had eaten all of the rest of the bread in her pack. She ate, and began to feel better.

For a few moments, her thick wool skirt spread around her in the snow like a dark blue pool, she closed her eyes and touched at her memory of the night before. But like a true nightmare, it had ceased to have the power in the day that it had in the night. Indeed, her feeling was one of cautious relief. She felt as if she had undergone a test, and while the final results were not yet in, completing it was enough for now.

"Where to now?" she said, getting up and shaking off a powder of snow from her clothes.

Oh, west, said the voice.

It sounded happy, so she knew there was not far to go.

*

It is impossible for sorcerers to run into each other, in the literal meaning of the term; they always know where they are. But Lhennuen and the other Siol found themselves standing at either side of a clearing thick with snow, and while she could not speak for his feelings, she at least was surprised. How many Siol were there in the world? And to meet one here—

"Peace," she said.

The other sorcerer made a gentle bow in return. Lhennuen hesitated, unsure. Hena etiquette was precise, and none more so than the Siol's. That was not the proper response.

But no part of the etiquette involved shouting across a distance. Well, if he wanted to fight, she could best him.

She began to cross the clearing towards him, her skirt and robe scraping trails in the snow as her feet sunk lightly into the crust. Before she had gone a few strides he approached her in turn, his movements loose and youthful beneath a tatty grey robe, which flapped over an equally tatty fur coat. His face showed restrained care.

"Asturyelni khaba," she greeted him formally in Hadra. She bowed the bow to equals, touching her forehead with the fingers of her right hand, to show him the family tattoo on the back of her hand. She was suddenly self-conscious of the fact that she was not wearing her headscarf. She had not expected to meet anyone, much less a man. But all she could do was hope that he would ask nothing forward.

"I am Siol Lhennuen Hegaantendre Damaiud e Kasith, Belim Hadheran."

When she rose, she expected a greeting and an introduction in return. She received only the bow. He too touched his forehead with his hand; but to her immense surprise she saw that the back of his hand was without either tattoo or scar. Was he Seianshe—a far-northerner? But his hair was brown, not blonde; nor did he have the round chin of a Seianshe. He was certainly Hena. But either he had never been tattooed as an adolescent, or he had removed it with magic. She was intrigued. A story there, either way.

He dropped his arm and rose with a dancer's grace. She thought perhaps that he had been lightly mocking her gesture; or just copying it with skill; there was something off, too loose-jointed about his body language. Hena and yet not Hena.

Her eyebrows were already on the way up at these conundrums; but when he gently touched his mouth to say that he could not speak, they shot up all the way to her hair. A Siol who was mute? And yet so much of magic was song.

If he was offended by her surprise, he did not show it, but gestured that she come closer. As she did, slightly wary and holding a spell of protection in abeyance, he stooped and drew something in the snow. She expected writing as she looked down, but didn't find it. What she saw was nevertheless clear. A sketch, in a few striking lines.

"A bird? Bird? That's your name?" She used the Henanue word, *Huo*.

He looked at her. The taste of intuition under her tongue made her say: "Yugho. It's the Hadra, isn't it." Of course, the Siol's language.

He nodded. Something that surprised her passed over his face: intense relief. She could see his wariness vanish from his posture like a cloak dropping to the ground, being replaced by released exhaustion as he looked at her. She understood then that he had not been able to communicate with anyone for a very long time.

She smiled. "If your name is Bird, do you like to fly?"

His face broke into a childish smile and he nodded.

"Me too," she said. "Either as a hawk—or a dragon."

He grimaced suddenly as if he disapproved. She was startled, afraid she had offended him. Holding her eyes with his own, he stretched out his arms to either side, and even before the motion was finished, he was a small grey sparrow, at first falling daringly through the air, and then catching himself with the wind under his stretched-out wings. He swooped past her and then away in a long arc, making her spin, laughing with surprise, to watch him.

"Very nice," she said with a grin, as he came to rest on a branch nearby. "I promise not to hunt you, when I'm a hawk."

He lifted from the branch and flew a corkscrew, then landed gently, in a poof of snow, as a man once more. He looked at her again disapprovingly.

"I *am* a hunter," Lhennuen said, "by nature. But I choose what to hunt."

He tipped his head back in acknowledgment, though he would never give his approval. There was something too gentle about him to ever approve of blood.

"And you hunt too, I imagine, if you live out here in the winter. Or do you Gate somewhere to buy food?"

Yugho shook his head, as if the idea were distinctly unappealing. He spread out his hand over his heart, then abruptly clenched it into a tight fist, to show his weapon of choice. There was sorrow in his face, as if he regretted even those bloodless means of murder.

"Oh, I see. Well, that's tidier than my way, for sure."

As she said so, Lhennuen realized she had assumed he lived in the woods. Perhaps he was merely passing through; perhaps he lived in a village or even a city. But as she tried to weigh those possibilities, she suspected that her assumption had been more than an assumption. Call it a guess based on his lack of a tattoo: or call it something more.

"You live out here?" she said.

He nodded. His shaggy, knife-cropped hair flopped onto his forehead.

"Alone?"

A nod again.

Lhennuen paused, stretching out her senses. He was not

closing his mind to her. She could not read his thoughts, but if she were to guess what he was thinking, she would always be right. Even she found it a little unnerving.

She might have asked him if he served a village, or some villages; but the idea was unthinkable to her, and so she had her answer already. Instead she said:

"You want to be left alone." It was not a question.

Yugho looked at her. His eyes were dark grey, darker than his robe, and full of doubt. He hesitated on the edge of a nod.

"Do you want me to go?" Lhennuen asked him in a low voice. For a moment she did not have her usual confidence.

Yugho shook his head "no," after a second's thought.

Lhennuen was not sure what to say. She thought she had come out here to be alone. But of course it was not as simple as that: nothing is. At last she said:

"I also appreciate the value of being alone. But not, perhaps, without friends to be alone with."

His face gentle, he reached out. She startled, too used to Hena ways, but his fingers brushed only the edge of her spell of warmth and not her sleeve. He completed his motion with a gesture: Follow me.

*

He showed her his home with pride. It was better-built than she had expected: There was enough of the wild in him that she would not been surprised had he lived in a cave. But it was a rough log cabin set in a small clearing, with a smooth plank floor in the single room, a bricked hearth and chimney, and a lean-to on one side that served as a cellar. Yugho threw wood in the hearth and had it alight in a second with a puff of his breath and a gesture of his hand.

"You didn't build this," said Lhennuen, sitting cross-legged next to him on the floor. He had given her the single blue-checked pillow, which was ragged beyond belief. She was looking over his shoulder at the windows, which had uneven glass in them. If Yugho had made them with magic, he would have done better.

Yugho shook his head no.

"Inherited it?" she tried.

No.

Lhennuen fell silent, not knowing how to find out the story. Then she accepted that she would never know, and closed her eyes for a moment, enjoying the heat of the fire on her face. She let her warmth spell ease away, and felt relief. It was a weight she hadn't noticed until it was gone.

Yugho scrambled around to prepare a pot of herbal tea, and when it was ready he sat beside her in front of the fire. Having given her the single floor-pillow, he sat on a thick rag rug. Lhennuen noticed that he was drinking from a soup bowl while she received a cup (his only). But she did not comment.

After she had finished her first cup and he had refilled it, he leaned forward and caught her eyes. A small gesture towards her: *you.* And a gently circling hand: *hereabouts.* And a rising hand: *why?*

Lhennuen took another sip from her cup and rested it on her lap, cradled between her hands. She looked into the fire for a second. But there was nothing to say but the bare truth. She looked at him.

"Well," she said, "my husband just died."

Yugho's face was stricken. In a single graceful motion, he drew himself up onto his knees, and bowed, stretching both hands toward her; then rose from his bow while covering his face with his hands.

"Thank you," Lhennuen said. "Thank you very much, Yugho." After a pause, she said, with a crooked smile: "You express grief much more elegantly than I can. But don't let it hurt you too much; I did most of my grieving when I married him, knowing what would happen. And he made his peace with it a long time ago. It's...a relief, in some ways, to have it over and done with."

She would have said that to almost no one on earth: certainly not Hapato. But she had no doubt that it was safe to say it to Yugho. He was, like her, not entirely human, and would not be shocked.

Yugho understood, and made a silent "ahhhh." Then he looked at her uncovered hair. She caught that question which he did not ask.

"'Just,' " she said. "Yes, 'just.' But I couldn't wear it. I love him, I miss him, but I'm...changing."

Yugho made a gesture that was the opposite of the one he had made earlier. A fist, suddenly opening outwards and rising up. She watched.

"Free," she said. "Yes. Something like that. I hope he'd understand....Or if not understand, at least forgive me. He knew who I am." He was peering at her, asking a question. She laughed softly and sipped from her cup. "I've always been free," she said. "That is both the reason for and a result of my power as a Siol. But when you're free you've no one to answer to but yourself and God, and that's...where I am now. So I've come here to—do what you're doing, really. Sit in silence, and fly, and talk to God."

Yugho was looking at her face. He put his bowl down, rose with grace, and walked to the bedmat. Lhennuen twisted to watch him.

Then, quick as a sparrow, he whisked the blanket off the bed, twisted it around himself, and sat on the floor. Meeting Lhennuen's eyes, he reached over and patted the bed firmly.

Lhennuen burst out laughing.

"You are a good man, Yugho. But—"

But what? She stopped laughing. It was not for nothing that she had met this man today. It was obvious that she was supposed to—learn from him, teach him, love him, hate him, hunt him; be his neighbor, his friend, his enemy. Something. She didn't know what lesson she was being taught; but she felt her way through, trying to find the path towards, if not the answer, at least the question. She had intended to build her own hut—and still intended to. But that would take days, and it would be nice to have a warm place to sleep in the meantime.

When in doubt as to what God's asking, she thought, say "yes." It might go horribly wrong, but at least you'll have gotten into trouble honestly.

Yugho was looking at her intently.

"It *is* dreadfully fortuitous, isn't it?" she said.

Yugho was surprised: then he grinned. He bowed.

"Well," she said after thinking about it, "I'll stay for a bit. But you must tell me when I've overstayed my welcome."

He shook his head.

"Very nice of you to think so. But we've only just met—so it may be wise to withhold your judgment."

When Lhennuen woke at dawn the next morning, she found that Yugho was already awake, and had been so long enough to run an errand: there was a second, newish bedmat beside the first, and a second bowl taking shape in Yugho's hands as he worked a piece of wood by the fire. Lhennuen snorted and pulled the blanket back up over her head. She had no desire to get into an argument before the sun was over the horizon.

Yet the argument, when they had it, consisted of Yugho shaking his head "no" to her inquiries about where he thought she ought to build her own cabin. She walked out on her own, following the stream that ran through one side of the clearing, found nothing promising, and returned to the cabin just before a snowstorm began. It lasted all night and did not stop. She could have sent it elsewhere, but she dug shriveled vegetables out of the lean-to and helped make supper, instead.

*

It snowed for four days.

"Is this usual?" she asked, rubbing the window to look out. The snow was past the sill.

Yugho nodded. He had finished with the bowl and a spoon and was working on sanding and oiling a cup to complete the set.

Lhennuen paced from one side of the cabin to the other in a swish of skirts. The cabin was small and her stride rapid; it took her three steps in each direction. She was alive with anticipation at getting outside, in conditions other than a blur of snow.

Yugho, it seemed, had the ability to meditate silently for days on end. She had managed to join him for the last four days, with no exercise but collecting firewood, but it had used all of her willpower to keep her sanity in doing it. The inside of her own mind did not interest her particularly; God was being silent; and wallowing in loss was not something of which she was capable. (She tried it for a few minutes, and heard Davrith's voice in her ear: "Oh, knock it off, 'Nuen, you know better." And she'd laughed out loud, startling Yugho.)

She'd been taught as a priestess that differing types of meditation suited differing temperaments. Yugho could sit. But she had to move, or, failing that, study. God, in her experience, often spoke to her through books.

It was a choice she'd made, not to Gate out. A large part of that was that she had been taught unequivocally never to draw a sword inside, and she could not bring herself to overcome her training without good reason. And also, it would be rude to Yugho, her host.

Another reason was that she'd been challenging herself.

She finished her second turn back and forth between the hearth and the window, and then went abruptly to kneel in front of Yugho. He looked up from his work.

"Am I staying?" she said, dropping all of the carefully constructed questions she'd considered over the last four days. He was far wiser than she, and she felt that she would fail him if she asked anything that did not cut straight to the heart.

Yugho's face gentled. He smiled.

"But you mustn't fall in love with me, you know," Lhennuen said.

Yugho's smile quirked. Not becoming less than a smile, but turning from an expression of pleasure to one of humor and rue.

Lhennuen looked at him. Then she said,

"Oh, to hell with *that*," disgusted with the weakness of men. She scrambled to her feet. "I'll be back after sunset, probably."

*

She owned a fur coat, but it was many years old and collecting holes. More importantly, it was at her temple, and she could not think of a way to get it without being seen. Therefore she decided to Gate, not to any place she went often, but to the capital city Avven, where even a Siol could do her shopping with only a little remark.

The middle-aged couple fondling each other in the alleyway where she stepped out were a bit surprised to see her. Or maybe it was the smell they were surprised at; the Heina were a tidy people. She headed to the public bath first, before seeking a meal that consisted of something other than root vegetables. If Yugho could not find in the woods or grow it in his garden to stow for the winter, he didn't eat it.

She restrained herself mightily in the shops and returned home (funny how easily she thought of it as "home") with only a coat, a bundle of six books, a grease lamp and a bar of soap.

*

It snowed and snowed and snowed again. When it was not snowing too heavily, Lhennuen would hunt, as a hawk, or, for a change, as a muscular lynx with shaggy spotted pelt and black-tipped ears. Or if the catch of the day before had been enough for a while, she would walk, in no particular direction, simply listening to the birds, and to the trees, and to God if It wanted to chip in. Yugho occupied himself separately, disappearing for the day and returning when night fell, often bearing a limp hare or vole or bird of his own.

When it snowed, and Yugho sat, she read. Mythology; travelogues; history; religion; textbooks on many a varied subject. The first six books lasted as many weeks and had to be swapped back to the bookseller in Avven for new ones.

In the endlessly long evenings, they talked. Yugho disclaimed the ability or perhaps the desire to read or write (which she found impossible to believe, if he were a Hena) but she had come to understand his wide vocabulary of gestures, and she could often pick from the air images enough to patch stories and opinions together. He would not speak of his past life, doing nothing but shrug when she asked; but they talked of hers, sometimes, of Davrith and the eccentricities of her family, which made Yugho laugh silently; and he told her how he had spent his day, in play with a fox he had befriended, or getting cussed at by a family of grouse, or breaking his own record at skipping stones. And she would read to him bits from her books, on Tabogai culture or the classification of trees by leaf-shape, and they would discuss that until the fire had burned down too much for her to see his expression.

After three or four months, snug at home under a drift of snow, they started sleeping together. She didn't love him in the same way she had loved Davrith. But why would she?

*

"*This* isn't usual, is it?" she said, when spring came seemingly overnight. They shed their fur coats and the roof shed its bed of snow. The drifts melted in a week of steady warmth, the stream swelled to three times its size, and buckets of slush came in the door until they magicked it out.

It wasn't usual, but it was welcome. No longer having to hold a spell to keep from freezing, they felt lighter, mental space being rediscovered that had been forgotten. Yugho gleefully played drums on tree stumps. Lhennuen built a fire outside in a stone fire-ring she had not known was there beneath the snow, hung up a cauldron and boiled every scrap of clothing they owned. Together they made repairs to the battered cabin, working the wood with magic rather than tools. The inside too they scrubbed out, ceiling to floor. Lhennuen splurged in Avven to have a new dress made, while ripping up the one it would replace in order to make fresh floor-pillows.

The morning after their spring cleaning was finished Yugho went out, giving her a kiss and making the gesture that said he would bring home dinner, good hunting willing. Ordinarily she would have gone out her own separate way, but today she stayed in to read, lounging lazily on the bedmat with a book of travel stories. She read until lunch, during lunch, and after lunch, until she was startled to high alert by the alarm of her sixth sense, just seconds before she heard hoofbeats and a voice shouting:

"*Siol!*"

She had already dropped the book; she swooped up her sword in a single motion as she bolted for the door. She threw it open.

The girl had just leapt from her horse. He was small and shaggy; she was as slender as a leaf, and young enough that her hair was cut short and her legs clad in work trousers rather than a proper dress. She dropped her reins on the ground and made to dash the last ten yards for the cabin. But she caught sight of Lhennuen standing in the doorway and came to as quick a halt as if she'd run into a wall.

"What's the matter?" Lhennuen said, coming forward. "You called for a Siol?"

The girl looked at her with huge, astonished eyes. "Oh—so *you're* the one he got the bedmat for!"

Lhennuen was caught up short, and she felt herself blush. Her stride faltered. But she said firmly: "Right. I'm his lover. Who are you?"

Remembering herself, the girl dropped a sketchy bow. "Skoldi Gefeindre Soskulus e Herede. Are you a Siol too?"

Lhennuen did not point out that that was what the grey robe meant. "Yes. Have you—"

"Will you help us?" Skoldi choked on her words in her haste and fear. "We're flooded—the rivers always flood but this year we're going to be swept away—we've already lost—" She was very nearly crying; would have been, had she not been Hena. "*Can* you help us?"

"Yes, I can," Lhennuen said. "Your village is Herede, you said? Where is it?"

The girl nodded and took up her horse's reins again, going to his side to mount. "Come on, he can carry both of us—"

"Wait. I can Gate. What direction?"

The girl turned back to her, surprised. "North. Uh, northeast. You can really do that?"

"Yes, but I can only go to a place I've seen. I've walked north along the river about to—oh, there were three birch trees in a perfect triangle at the edge of a pebble beach on the west bank, and an island out in the middle—"

The girl's eyes glowed. "That's close! But the beach'll be underwater now."

"If I put us in the forest west of it, how do we get there?"

The girl bit her lip so hard it bulged red. "Just follow the river north. But the main part of Herede is on the east bank...and I'm sure the bridge is out by now."

Lhennuen nodded. "All right. In that case, I'll go, you'll stay here. You'll be safe."

"No! I want to—"

"At this point you can't help, other than by being safe. You'll stay here. Yugho will be home in a couple of hours; all you have to do is tell him what happened."

"Yugho?" the girl repeated. "You mean—Bird? I have to stay with him?"

Her expression told Lhennuen more about Yugho's interactions with the locals than any speech ever could have. Dislike, doubt, need, a little fear, but no outright terror. Not that she had expected that.

"For a while." Lhennuen's voice softened. "He's—good, you know. I think he's just a little afraid of people." Then she ordered: "Turn your horse the other way. He might be frightened."

She'd had her scabbard and sword belt loose in her hand by her side to not be threatening; now, she buckled it around her waist. Skoldi backed off, herself frightened, but living with it. She turned her horse, looking back over her shoulder.

Sword drawn, Lhennuen stood with her eyes closed, rapidly flicking through scattershot memories of a walk she'd taken only twice. She'd not done it again after seeing a boat on the river and realizing she didn't want to meet anyone. But thankfully, the memory did not have to be clear: it just had to exist.

Singing, she raised her sword and sketched three lines and then a circle in the air with it, swinging its point as high as she could reach. The spell was an easy one for her and was done in only a few lines of song. She sheathed her sword.

"Where is it?" said the girl doubtfully.

"It's here," said Lhennuen, who could see the shining loop as if it had been painted on the air. "Help yourself to some stew. And have faith."

And she stepped through the loop into another woods, where the trees were the same but their pattern was different. And there was a roar not too far away, from the furious river.

*

She'd told Skoldi to have faith; Lhennuen too had to have faith, in her own untested skill as a water engineer. As soon as she had closed her Gate she took a bird's form, rising as swiftly as she could over the trees so she could see the river. It was hard, as a hawk, to shake free from a hawk's little brain. Thinking of what spells she might soon use was impossible. But she could observe, and remember for later.

Even as a hawk, she was startled by what had happened to the river. The last time she'd seen it, it had been a peaceable if icy flow of green, with pebble beaches here and there along its banks. She'd thought it might be a pleasant place to swim, in the summer.

But not even the most foolish of souls would swim in it now. It had tripled in breadth, increased ten times in speed: drowning the beaches and scouring the trees that should have been far above the waterline. It had ripped down many in its path, and their bodies swirled and dashed with the raging current, along with clots of brush that were visible one moment and submerged beneath the white water the next.

She flapped her wings, gaining height; then, with a single shrill cry, flew north. Raindrops slid away over her feathers.

*

The village was in even worse straits than she'd expected. In their valley among forested hills they had not one river to contend with, but two: a second came down around a hill to connect with the first, and near the base of the hill, within the fork of the two rivers, was the village proper. Usually, she thought, it would be far enough up-slope that it would be safe from any normal flood. But this was no normal flood. She took a low turn around the area, banking her wings.

It was immediately apparent that some buildings along the bank of the east-to-west river had already been ripped away. And the banks of the north-to-south river were simply no longer apparent: the entire narrow plain to the west of the village was flooded. A few large *birevo*, family houses, were scattered at the westernmost edge of what had been the plain. The closest to the river was already flooded beyond repair, the others sandbagged with varying degrees of success.

That was troublesome. The easiest way to protect the village would be to shift the course of the larger river westwards, away from the village; but with those houses there, that would cause too much damage. Moreover, they probably needed the plain as grazing land during the summer.

She looped over the main body of the village. There were no more than a dozen structures, large shambling birevo and a few shops and workshops and a hall, most clustered together at the base of the hill. A levée had been built of sandbags, along the side of which water was already high. The current was somewhat slower here than it was downstream, as the river lost force in spilling over into the flat fields to the west; but nevertheless it did not seem right to her that such a rough construction would survive for more than a few minutes the battering it was receiving. Something rubbed inside her mind, like a grit of sand in a shoe. She gave another cry, the voice of which was lost in the roar of water.

She canted down, timing her drop so that she returned to her natural form just a few paces from the people standing beside the sandbag wall, a blacksmith's yard at their backs.

There were three of them—a lanky man in late middle age with tightly curled dark hair and a sharp-featured, unhandsome face; a woman with a voluptuous figure and a darkly tanned complexion; and a giant bear of a man with an unfashionable ruddy beard. The woman, oddly, had already had her head tilted up to watch Lhennuen come in, as if she knew that the hawk was more than a hawk. The two men followed her gaze and were in time to catch Lhennuen's transformation. They were all sopping wet in the light but steady rain.

As Lhennuen took her second step on the muddy earth, the irritated sensation exploded in her mind into knowledge, and she was blinded by the electric lavender light of a magician's tremulous magic, which was shoring up the sandbags, then flowing into the body of the young dark woman.

"Seddes defend!" said the lanky man involuntarily. The woman said nothing, her eyes observing but her mind too occupied to create speech. The big man turned pale and took a step back, raising his hand.

"You needn't make a warding sign at me," Lhennuen said. She had to raise her voice to be heard over the rush of the water. "I've come to help you, if I can. I was fetched by Skoldi Gefeindre Soskulus."

"Skoldi's well?" said the big man, his voice urgent. Lhennuen caught a certain family resemblance to the girl, in the ears that stuck out too far.

"She's well. I told her to stay at our cabin where she'd be safe."

The big man nodded, relieved but still a little frightened.

"So then you're not—" said the lanky man, then hesitated, as if over something awkward. He finished too low. "You're not the one who usually...."

Lhennuen said only, simply, as she had to Skoldi. "No. That's Yugho. I live there too now. I'm his lover."

"Oh," he said, relaxing. Changing one's sex was something beyond myth. Lovers were something dreadfully mundane.

The woman let out a sharp little crack of a laugh and said in a strained, distant voice: "She's the one he bought the bedmat for."

She had an accent. Lhennuen looked at her suddenly, seeing what she was for the first time. She wasn't merely dark-complexioned: her face, her body was different, shorter and curvier.

She was Tsiani.

For a half a second only, Lhennuen froze in surprise, staring at her. The woman looked back with aware but glazed eyes, as if she were doing complex sums in her head.

It wasn't that Lhennuen had never met any Tsiani; or even that she hated them. Not all of the Tsiani kingdoms were at war with the Heina, and there was a small but not negligible flow of traders in and out through uncontested areas of the long border. In Avven and other large cities, they were common and tolerated sights, though they were not encouraged to settle.

But *here*. To find a Tsiani, in a territory so northerly that in another hundred miles Seianshe would be herding reindeer; in a village so small that the only trade was likely bearskins and fish for wheat and wine?

Lhennuen's lips parted to say something, to ask a question. Then she stopped. There were far more important things to be dealt with.

"I'm going to work under your spell," she said to the woman. "It may hurt, though I'll try not to let it. I need you to hold on until your spell is broken. When it breaks, let go fast and get out.

You Made My Heart a Hunter

All right?"

"Yes," the woman muttered, withdrawing into herself as her fragile spell sapped her strength moment by moment. Lhennuen knew what that was like, holding up a spell while surviving only on the hope that someday you will be able to stop.

"I know you're exhausted. I'll go as fast as I can," Lhennuen said. She plucked knowledge out of the air, and turned to the big man. "You're her husband? Hold her hands. Hold her. Keep her warm."

Turning, Lhennuen caught the eyes of the lanky man. He was the mayor, she knew suddenly.

"Wait," she said to him. Just that. But he looked at her, and nodded. Work now, introductions later.

Lhennuen faced the river. She drew her sword out of her scabbard and rested its point in the mud. The wall of sandbags, which came up to her chin, was far too delicate a thing to touch directly with the sharp, focused magic that would flow through the sword. Even this more subtle magic, crawling with her mind up inside the structure laid over with the harsh bright shards of a magician's spell, was painful, like a scraping sound in her inner ear. She had to slide under the woman's spell without touching it, for it was stretched so thin, and had been held so long, that it would shatter at any disturbance. Even so, with what little contact she made, she could hear the other woman groan in pain. But she could not think of that now.

Lhennuen shied, too, from the thought of singing. She had to set the spell in place in her head, then activate it with only one word.

Keeping her eyes open so her mind would not be swept away by the water, she crept out in her thoughts through the wall of sandbags, where her words would usually have gone for her.

From here, the other woman's spell was a source of support around her. But the river was still cold and fast and horrible against one side of what was now her body, and she dispassionately found herself shivering with the fear of destruction and dissolution.

She moved along the wall, to the north, to the south, and to the east, along the second river, where the levée was already broken in some places and completely swept away in others. She marked what she could; then drew back into her own body and felt awareness flow back into her eyes. Yet the weight and shape of the levée was resting in her mind.

"*Vaille!*" she said. *Become.*

With little fuss, the entire levée *became*—a wall of concrete.

And the other woman's spell, all of her energy centered on something that no longer was what it had been, shattered and snapped—and Lhennuen caught the energy with her sword, which easily contained a magician's weak magic; and then she pushed it out again in a thread through the earth, where it flowed immediately back to the magician and was absorbed. She could sense the woman stamp her foot, a way to balance energy fast at the end of a spell that was broken.

Lhennuen turned. "Are you all right?" Her voice was hoarse, but she felt well. The rain, stopped for a while, was pattering down again with a sound like scattering grain.

The woman had half-collapsed into her husband's arms and was sobbing with dry eyes. The lanky man was near Lhennuen, hovering with a dozen unspoken questions, so she handed him her sword before he could be too surprised to take it, and went to embrace the woman.

"It's over," she said. With no thought, she balanced the woman's lavender energies with her own. The sobs caught abruptly in the woman's throat. She exhaled, and took a deep if shaky breath. Lhennuen drew away, letting space open up again between them, as it should be among strangers. She turned and took her sword from the lanky man, who had the quiet expression of an intelligent man faced with extreme happenings, who is forming no opinions until it's all over. She cleaned the mud off the tip of her sword with a flick of wrist and magic. Then it was back in its sheath and she could make an introduction.

*

The mayor was Aistra Isshainto Lotepadh. The big man was Hoei Madruanto Soskulus; and the Tsiani woman—and she was Tsiani, no mistake—was his wife, Tayitoös-Barema Soskulus. Tayitoös-Barema was leaning heavily on her husband, whose broad ruddy face was creased with concern. The Soskuluses excused themselves to make their way up the hill, tasked with instructions from the mayor to send down the rest of the village council now that it was safe. In the meantime Lhennuen fetched Skoldi and her horse.

She was grateful, in the eight paces between her Gate and the front door of the cabin, that Yugho had not returned. She was not sure what she would say to him. She was angry with him, something that had never happened before. The snow had been melting for over a week. Yugho had known of the village; he had to have known how badly it would flood this year. Even if he hadn't wanted to break his hermit's life, he could at least have told *her*.

She knew that she should've figured it out on her own. When the melt started she should have gone seeking those in need of help. But her anger at herself did not lessen her anger at

Yugho. It merely made it inexpressible, since his crime was worse than hers only by a matter of degree.

But when she closed her Gate, back in Herede, she closed off those thoughts as well. They would, unfortunately, keep.

She waited a moment while the mayor embraced and praised young Skoldi. After the girl was sent uphill to join the rest of the evacuees, Lhennuen said:

"I was thinking I would deepen the river."

The mayor's forehead creased. "I'm not sure exactly what you intend, my lady Siol."

Lhennuen pointed over the levée; the water was only a foot from the top. "Look. It's not slowing, and will likely still rise. I can't turn the river west because you've got those homes there. If I turn it to steam, there will still be more water coming downstream. But if I deepen the channel, the water won't rise so high. Once it's done, though, it's done for good. You know the land better than I. Is there a better way?"

"You *should* flood those houses," said a new voice. Lhennuen turned to see an older man with a salt-and-pepper moustache, who, in spite of his age, was compact and muscled from hard labor. He handed Aistra Isshainto a peaked leather cap to match the one he wore. When Lhennuen looked at him he bowed and introduced himself as Ereshezhu Farogento Fala. Then he continued what he'd been saying.

"They were built too damn close to the river in the first place. We have to sandbag them every couple of years and even then some of them are rotting. There's water lines on the walls, mildew in the wood. They're the homes of my neighbors and they're good people, but their ancestors were as dumb as chickens when they built those homes so close to the floodplain. Let the river have the whole valley if it wants. We have enough empty beds between us all, we can put up those families while we help them build new birevo up-slope."

"Well and good for *you* to say," protested another voice angrily. A handful of people had come downhill now. "You weren't born in one of those homes. My mother was born in that house right over there, and my mother's mother, and her mother's mother, who was a might sight brighter than a chicken—"

"They didn't flood when they were built," said another man in a soft voice. He looked as if he might be speaking from personal remembrance. "Things change. Even rivers."

"Besides," said a woman almost as old as he, "our birevos are at their bursting points taking in those who have already lost their homes. We'd have to start breaking up the families to squeeze everyone in. And that wouldn't do."

"Enough, everyone," said Aistra Isshainto. "Ereshezhu, we've already lost at least six buildings, probably eight. They certainly won't be rebuilt in the same places. But the Goamis and the Solaus don't deserve to have their homes destroyed as well, if they can possibly be saved. We barely have enough men to rebuild what's already ruined before next winter."

There were about twenty people in the blacksmith's yard now, and more straggling down the hill. The village council proper would be five people including the mayor, but no member of the council would ever make a decision without consulting their own heads of house. With the number of elders drawing around, it looked like no one wanted to have their opinion go unheard. Lhennuen could see a prolonged discussion coming, and on top of the fact that committees made her head throb, she did not think it a good idea to leave the houses on the west bank unattended until a consensus was reached. Whenever that happened.

"What were the options?" some newcomers wanted to know.

"Deepening the river channel is what came to mind," Lhennuen said. "Though I've no wish to act by fiat, that's what I'll do, unless you can come up with a better solution. This needs to be taken care of before the light goes." She finished quickly before anyone could interrupt her. "I'll leave it to you to discuss, while I see how I can help out on the other side of the river."

"The bridges are out," someone said.

"That is not a problem," she said. "I will be back shortly."

She turned into a hawk and flew across the levée, glad to escape before her head began to overheat from an overdose of talk.

*

The first and nearest birevo she didn't bother to investigate closely; indeed she would have gotten very wet if she'd tried. The water was up to the top of the first story windows, and it looked like a good chunk of one wing had been swept away.

The second and third homes she flew over—circling wide in hawk form—she didn't stop to examine either. Set close together, they were the farthest from the river. They were soggy, but they would survive.

At a glance, Lhennuen was unsure about the fourth home. Unlike the first home it appeared not to have any structural damage; but the brown floodwaters came four or more feet up its sides. She found a broken window on the second story and got herself inside with a well-timed dive. She regained her natural form in the middle of a bedroom.

For a second she stood still and looked around the room. There was only grey window-light to see by, but she could still see the bed and writing desk and empty clothes-hooks, stripped when the home had been evacuated. She picked a calligraphy brush off the floor and set it on the desk out of habit. She felt slightly unsteady, queasy, like the floor beneath her feet could not be trusted. Either too many changes between hawk and human, or—

She moved carefully out into the hallway, and down the stairs, seeing in the darkness by dint of a blue witchlight. The smell of mold overpowered her. She reached for her headscarf to cover her nose, didn't find it. With a grimace, she held the loose sleeve of her robe over her face instead.

Half-way down the stairs her witchlight broke out over a large room, casting a faint illumination into a hall of shadows. She stopped and peered down, clutching the banister and a spell. The stairs ended in water.

She extended her consciousness out to gently touch the walls. They gave when she touched them, spongy and slippery to her mind's touch. She shuddered. For a few moments she forced herself to examine the wood of the home, making sure that it was all as far gone as it appeared to be. But as soon as she was sure, she turned quickly and went back up the stairs, trying not to notice how they gave a little under her feet.

She wasn't sure what spell she would use if the house came down around her. The mental construct of becoming a fish was beyond her ability to summon easily; indeed the idea rattled her. Water was *not* her element.

As she stepped down the hallway towards the open door to the bedroom, there came a surprised shout and a pop of awareness at the same instant. At the far edge of Lhennuen's light she caught a movement; and her mind's eye was splashed with a bolt of energy like white paint thrown on glass.

"Ah!" Lhennuen said, startling backward and instinctively

raising an invisible spell-shield.

"Who the hell are are you?" blasted a voice from down the corridor.

Lhennuen flicked a hand upwards and her light expanded. She could see amidst the flickering shadows a very old woman with a small bow, arrow nocked. Lhennuen had not been able to see her at first, but she had certainly been able to see Lhennuen, lit up like an aurora.

"What are you doing in my house? You are no guest of mine!"

"I am not," Lhennuen said. She bowed. "I am a Siol, and I've come to help your village with the flood. I am here in this house, under the mistaken impression that it was deserted, to see how bad the damage was."

"You've come to help with the flood, huh? Where were you a couple of days ago when we really could have used you?"

A very good question, thought Lhennuen; and it pained her. She took the Siol's policy of being truthful rather than diplomatic.

"That is a very good question," she said. "Let me answer it like this. I didn't know there was a village here until today, even though I should have. You didn't send anyone to Yugho for help until today, even though you should have. Shall we call the fault unscoreable?"

The old woman said "Ha," but didn't lower her bow.

"Girl," she said, "Siol or no, you're young enough to be my great-granddaughter. Don't be snippy."

Lhennuen was astonished. A great many responses passed through her head, all of which could be interpreted as snippy under various definitions. When she had collected herself, she said with as much politeness as she could muster,

"Ma'am, if you were my great-grandmother, then I would hope you would have enough good sense to let me help you from a house that will collapse as soon as it's struck by a single log."

"I'm not leaving my home."

Lhennuen considered.

"Then you're a fool," she said.

The end of the arrow twitched. "Did you call me a fool, you —"

"I'm leaving now," Lhennuen said firmly. "This house may make it through the night, or it may not. And if the house doesn't kill you, the mold's likely to make you sick. I could knock you out and take you with me, but I have no business doing so, since it's your right to die how you wish; and that is what I will tell your great-grandchildren when they ask me why I didn't bring you back with me. Consider however that right now the only reason why you are standing in a house rotting in five feet of rising water is pride. And pride is an immensely stupid reason to die."

The woman looked at her hard for a moment over the bow. She didn't move. Lhennuen shrugged, turned to take two steps into the bedroom with the open window, and then, very deliberately, broke her training by drawing a sword inside. It almost hurt to do so. She forced herself to forget that, and swung it in an arc, singing.

By the time the Gate was ready, the old woman had come to the door of the room, her bow and quiver hanging limp in her hand. Lhennuen stood back and gestured.

"You *are* a snippy little girl," the woman said, stepping forward with dislike in her face.

"But seem to be slightly less of a fool than you appear," Lhennuen said.

*

As Lhennuen had expected, a noisy discussion was ongoing in the blacksmith's yard. Her Gate was smart enough of its own accord not to open in the middle of a crowd or a wall, so she found herself a ways up the hill in the middle of the path. She paused for a moment, disoriented, until she got her bearings. The old woman, having passed through ahead of her, had already struck off down the road. Lhennuen closed the Gate with a certain twist of her hand and followed after, picking her way carefully between puddles.

The old woman was noticed first, perhaps because she shouted "Let me through!" when she reached the crowd. A cry of "Nazu Sasange!" went up as she was recognized.

"How did you get here?" they asked, echoing each other. "We thought you were drowned!"

"I decided it was time to come back," Nazu Sasange said without batting an eye. Lhennuen was not sure whether to smile or grimace. She stopped away from the edge of the crowd, making a judgment call that shoving her way through the knot of people gathered around the old woman would not be good for a priestess's dignity.

She waited for the clamor to die down. When it had, she said: "Have you decided?" in a carrying voice. The crowd quieted somewhat and those closest turned, noticing her presence for the first time. She met their eyes, waiting again.

There was a rustle of motion. A moment later the crowd parted and the mayor came through, followed by Ereshezhu Farogento and three other men.

"My lady Siol. We've argued; now we'll vote."

For the first time the crowd was truly quiet as everyone strained to listen. The council gathered in a small circle and voted several motions in rapid succession. It was four to one in favor of lowering the bed of the north-south river only for such distance as it flowed by the village. Hena law strongly preferred unanimous decisions, but in an emergency, four to one would suffice. They *were* unanimous about outlawing construction within a certain distance of the banks of either river; but failed to pass the motion to shift the smaller hillside river away from the village. Lhennuen was glad about that. She would have overridden that vote if it had passed, fiat or not. She had seen from the air that the buildings on its banks were destroyed, and she had no business rearranging a river to protect wreckage.

When they were done, Lhennuen said simply:

"All right. Please see that everyone has moved up the hill as far as possible and is on stable ground. There will likely be a small earthquake."

*

Instead of the transmutation she had done earlier, turning the sandbags into concrete, this was a spell of animation: asking the earth, deep down, to creep part of itself from *here* to *there*. That seemed better to her than disturbing the topsoil of the plain or the life of the river. The hill would be a little higher, the river a little lower, but her object was that no one but a native would be able to tell.

She finished singing just as the sun slid behind the forest, casting off a few sparks of orange light to color the grey clouds from beneath. The last thing she'd done was turn the levée into stones and gravel, which she sent sliding under the water. While still muddy and rapid, the river was a great deal less bloated now that it had a deeper channel. The village was safe.

Standing on the roof of the Solaus' house to the west of the flooded plain, she turned away from the river for the first time to watch the sunset. It was a beautiful sight but a cold one. She shivered once, hard, like a passing seizure.

Now, she thought wearily, came the hardest part. Going home. You could never use your last breath of strength in your spell. There was always that time after the spell was done, and you had to make your way to a friendly place, and accept congratulations or complaint, and sit up long enough to have something to eat, and find a place to sleep before you collapsed. That was the real end. How you went home after a spell was what showed your worth.

Lhennuen closed her eyes and pressed her hands over her face for one second. She wanted just to go back to the cabin and lie down next to Yugho's warmth and not wake up for days. But this was not even the hundredth worst exhaustion she had suffered in her life, perhaps not the thousandth. She had always gone on before and she would again now. She dropped her hands, and with only a little difficulty, slid one more time into the body of a hawk.

It was easy to see where most of the villagers had congregated; in spite of the fact that she had told them to get uphill, they had come down to get a better view, packing themselves down the paths of the village and at the the upper windows of the nearest birevo. Lamps and candles were being lit. As she flew she let her intuition to guide her to the mayor. She found him much where he had been before, holding a lamp aloft. She dropped neatly in front of him, changing into her human form without having to take a step to steady herself.

"It's done—" she began; but she was interrupted by a ragged cheer by the villagers who were near enough to see her in the dusk. She waited until they had finished.

"It's done," she said. "I'll come back tomorrow so I can get a good view, and see if anything needs fixing. And I'll see how I can help you with the rebuilding. But until then I'll bid you good night."

"You have the gratitude of all of us," said Aistra Isshainto with the deepest bow. They all bowed, in silence.

Another man stepped forward, holding up a lantern of his own, which cast just enough light to show that it was Hoei Madruanto Soskulus, and his wife with him.

"Come and have some soup before you go," said Tayitoös-Barema. Her voice was quiet. "The family Soskulus invites you to be our guest, as an inadequate expression of our appreciation."

Lhennuen hesitated. The offer of food was difficult to reject politely at the best of times. And it was not just Hoei and Tayitoös who were asking her; with that phrasing, the invitation came from the elders of the house of Soskulus. To refuse it without pressing reason would be insulting—although as a Siol she would be given the benefit of the doubt about the validity of whatever "pressing reason" she put forth.

Yet also, at the back of her mind, she was interested by the Tsiani magician, and the as-yet unknown stories which her presence implied....

What decided her, however, was the soup. Even if Yugho had caught something, the odds were good that it would need skinning and gutting and roasting before it could be eaten.

"I would be honored to accept the kind invitation of the family Soskulus," she said with a bow, "though I must apologize in advance that I am tired and will likely not make very interesting guest."

"It is not for interest's sake that we extend our invitation," Tayitoös said, still quiet.

Lhennuen nodded slowly. She appreciated the words.

She was escorted to the Soskulus birevo, where they were met by the house elders, the oldest man and woman of the line. They were gracefully shriveled, and extended their gratitude in the way Lhennuen most preferred: They bowed, said "Thank you," and left her alone. Lhennuen understood then that Tayitoös, the magician, had told them to do that. She was as appreciative as her tiredness would allow.

"Would you like to eat in the kitchen?" asked Tayitoös.

Lhennuen looked at her. Guests ate in the dining hall. Friends and family ate in the kitchen.

"I would be honored," she said.

They shed their coats in the warmth of the huge hearthfire. Tayitoös's gown was lavender silk to match the color of her magic; it was beautiful against her dark olive skin. Dinner was venison and parsnip stew with bread and butter and cheese, very simple and one of the better meals Lhennuen had ever tasted. It seemed the rest of the house had already eaten—or else Tayitoös had told them to go away—so she was joined only by the two.

"Just call me Tayitoös," said the Tsiani woman, when Lhennuen thanked her by her full name as was polite. "Barema, my father, is long dead—and had none of my love for a long time before that."

Lhennuen didn't know what to say. She nodded.

"You saved my wife's life, my lady Siol," Hoei said.

That was possible, so Lhennuen again said nothing, only looked at him. She wished she could praise Tayitoös's skill, which for a magician was indeed strong, but she thought it might come off as condescending. After a moment she said, "Your wife is brave to undertake what she did."

Hoei looked at Tayitoös. "She has always been a brave woman," he said with visible pride.

Tayitoös shrugged, reaching for another piece of bread. "Necessity demanded it."

That was a very Hena thing to say, and it was odd to hear it in a Tsiani accent. Lhennuen paused with her spoon in her hand. She was curious, and the soup had allayed her tiredness for a while; but she hesitated to ask, not sure how it would be taken. Finally she asked the Tsiani woman: "How long have you lived here?"

"Nine years," Tayitoös answered, meeting Lhennuen's eyes.

Lhennuen wasn't sure how to read her. Tsiani were in general more expressive and quicker to make friends than the Heina; but Tayitoös, while not at all unfriendly, was simply *quiet*. Was it her nature; or was it because Lhennuen was a stranger; or because they were Siol and magician, not two groups known for their mutual respect?

She took Tayitoös's even gaze to mean that further questions would not be rude.

"Will you permit my curiosity about how you came to live here?" Lhennuen said.

"Ah," exclaimed Hoei, "she fell in love with me, Gods know why!"

Lhennuen grinned. Tayiotoös smiled suddenly, without restraint.

"I did," she agreed, her reserve unraveling and falling away like thread from a dropped spindle as she looked at her husband with affection. "He had traveled to Emsofi to make a trade for wine; I was the niece of the vintner, and he took me home instead of the wine."

"She either fell in love with me," Hoei corrected himself, "or else she did a damn fine job of pretending, in order to get out of there. But why would she keep it up all these years—that's the question!"

"I was seventeen and unmarriagable," Tayitoös said, her voice scathing; "no Tsiani man would marry a magician. Women magicians, as we all know, are whores."

Lhennuen blinked.

"I won't say my uncle mistreated me," Tayitoös said, "but I was without status. If I could not marry and become a proper respectable woman, then I would be a cloistered virgin forever, trotted out only to verify the value of goods or mend a broken arm. The rest of the time I did not exist."

"So I stole her," Hoei said.

"So I convinced him to," Tayitoös said, with a flash of her dark eyes. "He brought me here, and I discovered a mind I didn't know I had."

"*I* always knew it was there," Hoei said complacently. "In fact she's smarter than I am. Why else would I go to the trouble, but to get someone who would tell me what to do?"

Lhennuen laughed.

Tayitoös smiled; then didn't. She looked serious.

"And is our curiosity permitted?" she asked, her voice gone quiet again. "Why are you here, Siol and priestess of Hadhera?"

Thinking, Lhennuen chased the last chunk of parsnip around her bowl with her spoon. Only when it was caught and swallowed did she answer.

"I was looking to find out what use I could be," she said at last. "Apparently, the answer is: building houses."

*

Even before the floodwaters receded, they began to scout for trees, seeking out those that were suitable for housebuilding. Lhennuen and the village's priest—a follower of Seddes—and Tayitoös were kept busy with that: Lhennuen and the priest in marking the trees with a sign of consecration once found, and Lhennuen and Tayitoös in felling them once marked.

Lhennuen settled into the pattern of work easily if not with great pleasure. She flew to the village early each morning and walked the forest alone until she had marked enough trees to make calling in the rest of the work team worthwhile. It was a somewhat monotonous task but it required enough care that Lhennuen could not allow her mind to wander. In that way it reminded her of being on patrol with the army.

The villagers were used to Tayitoös's magic, so they accepted Lhennuen's skills with enthusiasm, incorporating them into their plans as if they were merely new kinds of bricks and scaffolding. She spent endless days shifting logs from the forest to the first building site via Gate, until her arm ached from swinging her sword to open the Gate and her knuckles swelled from having spells knit tightly around them while she used her voice for other things. After the first week, she began to dream at night the six lines of the spell that she used to levitate the logs. They sang over and over in her ears and painted themselves on the insides of her eyelids under she awakened and forcibly replaced them with a prayer.

Working alongside the villagers reminded her of her army service in a different way as well. Again she was the sole woman among a group of men mostly older than she. In the army, where she had been indefinitely assigned to a unit, she had made an effort to make friends. It had taken her fellow soldiers a while to forgive her for being chaste, and too intelligent for comfort, and too powerful likewise; but she had protected them with cheerful efficient viciousness, deliberately stood on no dignities, and had a natural capability for black humor. So after a time they had accepted her. *Our* Siol.

It had looked easier from the outside than it had been from the inside—but that was true of a lot of things.

And, in that case, she had chosen the challenge. It was not for nothing that she served Hadhera, the goddess of war.

But in Herede: she took instruction punctiliously, remained silent in the midst of a hustle and bustle, and allowed herself to be used as an instrument by those with greater expertise. At the moment, that suited her.

She knew that they were curious about her, of course. She could see herself clearly through their eyes: a young woman who did not inhabit her youth, a soul held separate by the folds of a grey robe and a dignity that did not fear its own destruction. Standing quiet, she observed their curiosity and neither pitied it, nor was amused by it, nor felt the immediate need to appease it. And being Hena and well-brought-up, they asked her only what was respectful—news of the war and of trade and of the Autransis, which were like distant theatrics to them—and then censored each other to leave her to her silence. For she was a stranger, and a priestess, and most of a Siol, and those things were all due respect.

Sometimes she shocked them by laughing at their jokes. But it was her prerogative to not always be the same thing.

On occasion, Aistra Isshainto would come out with the work parties for an hour or two, observing with keen interest and assisting when he could. But one morning before the others came, he came to walk with her as he had not done before. She loosened her concentration on the trees and slowed her step.

"Mayor."

He was astute enough to hear the question mark on the end.

"My lady," he said, his step springy to match the animation of his hatchet-like face as he returned her look. "A question, if you'll consider it."

"Of course."

"Promise me you'll consider before you answer," he insisted.

Lhennuen raised her eyebrows and tipped her head in acknowledgment, if not exactly assent.

"My lady, what I—what we all want to know is—how can we repay you for this work you do? I know you don't *need* anything. But there might be something that would please you. Since you're helping us, let us care for you in return."

The corners of Lhennuen's mouth crinkled at his assumption that she would say she needed nothing. He was right. But she liked Aistra Isshainto; you could not dislike him. So she did make herself think for a moment before answering.

"I'm sorry to say I really do want just what Siol always want," she said at last. "Lunch. The option for dinner sometimes." She grinned, suddenly. "Pretty young men—No, I'm joking. I have one already." That was also a joke. Yugho was neither much pretty nor much young.

The mayor laughed. In the middle of his laugh, something occurred to her, and she said softly, "Ah!"

"What is it?"

"Maybe you could give me some information."

He half-bowed, still walking beside her. "If I can, I will."

She hesitated for a moment; then shook herself free of her

hesitation.

"About Yugho," she said.

"Who?...Oh. Bird."

"We communicate with each other...as well as you and I do. Or better. But...there are things he won't tell me. He speaks only of the present. And I..." She paused, and then because they were alone and she trusted him, she finished with the truth in an ironic voice: "I'm not sure I want to know—but I can never not ask."

They had stopped. Aistra Isshainto looked at her face closely, his features sharp and narrow as an ax blade, but his eyes gentle. She didn't quite meet them.

"Well," he said, "rest assured you gain no knowledge you'll have to struggle with. None of us knows more about him than you. When he came here four or five years ago, his hand was as unmarked as it is now, and his disposition even more skittish. In fact we met him only when a pair of our little ones got lost, and he brought them back. After that sometimes he would come to ask for a little salt or cloth, which we asked nothing for in return; but two or three times there has been something more than Tayitoös can handle, so we send for him. He comes, and then he goes, and he doesn't even stay for the dinner option or the pretty young women." He smiled. "Though now he has one."

Lhennuen gave a short laugh, and then still without meeting his eyes, turned to her path once more.

"That's all then," she said.

"Then I'll stop interrupting your work, for which you have a hundred thousand thanks. Good day to you, my lady."

Then he bowed, and was off lightly through the trees.

*

Yet Lhennuen did not like all of the villagers as much as she liked Aistra Isshainto. She had cause to revise her estimation of Nazu Sasange's foolishness: it was in truth boundless.

Nazu's initial dislike of her, as what she perceived as an upstart youth and an interloper, had increased to outright hatred when Lhennuen said that the Sasange birevo was beyond repair —and never mind that the village's two master carpenters both agreed. In Nazu's mind it was Lhennuen's fault, an opinion solidified when it was she who collapsed the house once and for all with a couple of words; though in truth a good kick would have done it.

Nazu was there to watch as it came down, standing tight-lipped at the front of the gathered crowd of her family and other villagers. Lhennuen saw her face but thought nothing of it. It was only after, when one of the council-members was giving Lhennuen his compliments on a tidy job, did Lhennuen hear Nazu's voice amongst the dispersing crowd. "As if she knows what it means to us," Nazu said to her family, bitter, meant to be heard. "She's got no family-home to lose, for she's got no family, has she? Or if she has, then she's no good to them: their birevo could collapse with all of them in it and she'd do nothing about it. Couldn't, for she's not with them."

Lhennuen caught her breath, and then forced it on again, normally. The council-member faltered in his speech, looked over Lhennuen's shoulder toward the backs of the departing Sasanges; then looked at Lhennuen. Lhennuen knew she had changed expression for one second and regretted that the man had seen it, but it couldn't be helped. She was not going to demand recompense of honor from the Sasanges, and so she was going to pretend she had not heard: and her hope was bent towards the fact that the council-member would be wise enough to do likewise.

He was. On her way home her lips moved soundlessly in a blessing on his name: even as her cheeks burned, and she cursed them for it.

And she hoped without faith that that would be the end of it.

*

While Lhennuen continued work with the priest and woodcutters in the forest, Tayitoös took charge of curing, by magic, the wood that had already been hewn, so that it dried and shrank now rather than after the house was built. Lhennuen saw her the day after the magician did the first batch, and was wrenched. The Tsiani's eyes were puffy as if she'd been crying, and she walked among the stacked, dry lumber with her back too straight as if she were afraid she might crumple otherwise. Lhennuen was at a loss to know whether she would give offense by sympathizing; by apologizing for not having done the spell herself; by saying she would do it next time; by noticing at all. As they inspected the lumber together with the head builder, she defaulted to the Hena way of pretending she saw nothing. Then the day moved on, and if she had been going to say something, the opportunity was lost in a blur of work.

*

After weeks of work they had enough lumber to begin building. It may have been because of the fuss Nazu kicked up at every opportunity; or it may have been, more sensibly, because the Sasange family was the largest whose house had been lost. Regardless of the reason, their birevo was the first to begin construction. Nazu was always there, watching each step as if she suspected a conspiracy of shoddy workmanship. She was there when Lhennuen inspected the foundation with the head builder. In the rain, it was dirty work by any method and when Lhennuen was done she absently flicked clean her skirt and robe with a short phrase that scattered the mud.

"Don't want to get your pretty posh embroidery dirty, eh?" Nazu cracked.

And Lhennuen could only blink, keeping her head turned away so as not to have to acknowledge the comment.

But then another insinuation, and another, each time they crossed paths. Lhennuen's fine clothes; the fact that she could never know the land as well as a local could; her relationship with a mute hermit "who can't argue back with 'The Lady'"; her dialect, which was either too Citified or too bookish (mutually exclusive things); even her strict silence in the face of Nazu's digs. Lhennuen could meet her ragging with equanimity, but not with good humor. She found herself avoiding the places Nazu was likely to be.

At least everyone else knew Nazu was an ass. Such was her position of elder of the largest family in the village that she could not be admonished outright by anyone but her head of house— but he, her brother, was quite literally deaf to the world. The head builder steamed and hissed to himself but could not forbid her to watch the building of her own home from the sidelines. The other workers—even many of those who were themselves Sasanges—closed their ears and subtly turned their backs, casting Lhennuen apologetic glances but unable to speak out. Aistra Isshainto did apologize, in private: "For all the good it does."

So if Nazu talked about Lhennuen behind her back, which Lhennuen could not imagine she would fail to do, Lhennuen felt reasonably safe that she was ignored.

Nevertheless she still had to bear what Nazu said to her face. Knowing Nazu was merely a fool, Lhennuen was not truly offended, but even though one does not take the whine of a mosquito personally, it still maddens.

And the restriction of her own response irritated her. It was her own choice, of course: she could have fought back, in private or in public. She could have called up the Sight to See what it was that twisted Nazu the way she was, and ravaged her with that knowledge. It was a victory she could easily seize, even without magic.

But any victory won by a priestess trained in logic and rhetoric over an uneducated countrywoman would be a hollow one. And it would have ended nothing; for to shame Nazu Sasange would be to incur the bitterest retribution.

The priestess of a goddess of war had to know what wars were proper to wage. That one wasn't.

So she stayed silent. When Nazu (again) called her a snippy little girl, Lhennuen blinked as if noticing her presence for the first time, and continued on her way. When Nazu implied she had chased her husband away with her coldness, Lhennuen just looked at her—and that look surely was cold. When Nazu, finally roused to a height by being ignored, accused Lhennuen in public of building a flaw into the Sasange birevo to bring about its collapse—a slur and a bad omen which so shocked the head builder that he opened his mouth to protest—Lhennuen said nothing more than: "The house is sound, madam, but you don't have to live there."

And finding Lhennuen too controlled to fight back, Nazu attacked willfully, and with the glee of a wicked child stomping ants.

*

Even when Nazu was not around, the work was tiring. At the end of the day—and they were long days indeed in the northern spring—Lhennuen was happy to fly home and eat what Yugho had caught, and talk and make love. There were holidays—new moons, an equinox, house-founding days, the days of gods local and official—on which the villagers would not work. She was always invited to their amusements and their feasts. She never went.

After two months the Sasanges' birevo was finished. There would be a feast, of course—held by the Sasanges. The brash, muscular forewoman of the second logging team came up to Lhennuen after the date had been set.

"Will I see you at the feast next week?" asked Dob Renni.

And in the question there was an uncertainty unsuited to a woman who had taken over a job considered strictly man's work just by dint of sheer personality. It was perhaps for that reason she had been the one nominated to ask, as the rest of the workers lingered around lunching and listening.

For a second Lhennuen looked at her. She could hear the silence of ears around them and suddenly wondered what object of mystery, what catalyst for talk and curiosity she was among these people. Then she gave a sharp laugh. She would not be Nazu Sasange's guest if hers was the last roof in the world.

"No," she said baldly, to all those ears. "And you know why."

Dob Renni opened her mouth.

"Don't," Lhennuen said, amused. If anyone would speak, it would be Dob. "It's pointless. I promise to come when the next one's finished."

Dob closed her mouth but still looked obstinate, as if she were planning how to protest. *It's your right to be there*, was what she was going to say; or maybe *But you have to stand up to her.*

"Don't," said Lhennuen again; and she laughed suddenly. She had got her small speck of vengeance against Nazu by declining to be her guest, even if no one else considered it that way; and it was satisfying. Dob gave her a look of scrutiny, as if wondering if she'd lost her mind.

But Dob let it drop at last. "I'm sorry I won't see you there."

"Better bread and eggs in the woods with good company, than a feast—" Lhennuen said cheerily, and left it at that.

*

Lhennuen returned to the village the day after the Sasanges' house-blessing, and found everyone hung over. Even days later, the party was still the talk of the village; or so she gathered, from the number of excited conversations that dried up as soon as she came near. She was amused by this, though not sure whether she ought to be.

She was sitting on a stone wall at the edge of the next construction site two days after the party, a rare moment of rest as she waited for the builders to need her. The flat popping sound of pegs being hammered was muffled by steady rain. Water was crawling under her collar. She was not thinking about much at all, except perhaps the sense-memory of water sliding off dark feathers.

"Hey, my lady," said Hoei, the diffident bear. She turned as he sidled up beside her. He had on a comically large hat. Lhennuen had a sudden vision of Tayitoös putting it on a pole and using it as an umbrella.

She wiped the rain from her eyes and smiled at him. "Hey, Hoei Madruanto."

"Tea?" he said, offering her a tea-bowl. "I'm afraid it's a little rained-in...."

"Tea would be lovely. Rained-in or not."

She took the bowl carefully from his large awkward hands and held it up beneath her face where the faint steam would warm her. Rain made the surface shimmer.

"So how was the party?" she said.

"Oh, it was great!" said Hoei expansively—slow on the uptake. "They slaughtered a bull, and even got *fruit* from somewhere—can you believe that? I had part of a—I was told it was called an 'orange.'" It was a Tsiane word, borrowed; he pronounced it with care. "Have you ever had one?"

She had had a bowl of them, and peaches and pears and things she didn't know the names of, as a girl visiting the court of the Autransis with her mother. Even at twelve, not yet a woman or a Siol, she had been hard to impress. The court had been interesting on an anthropological level. But those oranges had enraptured her.

"I have. A long time ago."

"The dancing was great. My girl, she can make even a big beast like myself look good." He sighed happily. "You should have been there! You're a young gal, you probably like to dance. You should have talked your boyfriend into coming."

She smiled.

"Usually I play the *kanna* at parties. Not very well, mind you—but I can keep a rhythm going."

The kanna was an instrument with a big belly, long neck, and deep voice to match. It was large enough that playing it, embraced between your legs and arms curled around it to pluck or bow the strings, was almost like dancing. In spite of her truthful assertion that she did not play very well, Hoei looked impressed.

"The kanna! Someone's got one of those somewhere...." He gave wracked his brain for the kanna's possessor, trying out a few names as an experiment before at last landing on: "Family Opei! They've got it. Talta Opei used to play before his hands got too stiff. I'm sure they'd let you borrow it, if you wanted to —"

Lhennuen was going to laugh at his enthusiasm; then she caught herself, because she had not played in ages, and she missed it. Then before saying, "A good idea—I might ask them," she checked herself again, because Hoei would take that as a call to have the kanna delivered to her before the night was out, with a ribbon around its neck. Hoei was impossible not to smile at.

"Maybe," was all she said.

*

The next house—the Laupita family's—was smaller than the Sasanges', and as much of the wood had already been cut, it was finished more quickly than the last. To Lhennuen it was just work. She came in the mornings and did what was needed. Finding the trees. Forming the foundation of concrete in the same way she had formed the levée. Raising the frame for the carpenters to assemble. Sometimes in the rain, sometimes in crisp spring sun. She came to know the areas of the village where Nazu Sasange spent time, and avoided them.

Her real life was elsewhere. It was in the forest, hunting, as a hawk or a lynx. Or just walking. Or curled up on a pillow with books around her, avidly reading Mezheir legends of questionable provenance, or on the building of aqueducts, as Yugho skinned a rabbit on the other side of the fire.

Yugho. Her real life was with Yugho.

She knew no more about his history than she did the first day they had met. At first, curiosity about his past had overwhelmed her. But over the months they spent together, she had come to accept that she never would know. Whatever his life had been, whatever had caused him to remove his clan tattoo, truly did not matter. He was a creature of the present: and for right now, so was she.

After all, she had come to the forest to let go some of her own past, too. And until God saw fit to answer her questions, her future was counted strictly in the building of houses.

She could not begrudge Yugho his silence, or his choices.

So she knew how he would answer, when she accepted a commission from the villagers to ask him something.

"The Laupitas' house-blessing is tomorrow," she said to Yugho one evening. "I have been told to invite you."

He raised his head from spooning up their stew, and gave her a look. Faintly incredulous, faintly humored. And some of that feeling he would never express. He did not need to shake his head to make his answer.

"Yes, I know," she said with a smile. "But I promised to ask."

He nodded.

They ate. After a while she said, "I'm not sure whether to wear my robe or not. What do you think?"

He sat back and pursed his lips. He set down his bowl with just a piece of gristle in the bottom. For a moment he was still, and then he raised his hands and swiftly expressed: *It depends on what you want.*

"It changes things, doesn't it?" she said. "I want to acknowledge their celebration. But—"

It becomes an obligation, he expressed, with a sharp drawing-in of his fist for the last word. The same motion he used for "binding." *From then on.*

He always understood what she meant. To go without the grey robe that marked her as a Siol was to change her relationship with the villagers; to invite something more than the professional. And done once, it was not something she could easily go back on. She wasn't ignorant of the fact that good things could come of it; but as Yugho had said, if she invited intimacy, it would become an obligation, expanding in small ways over time. And she felt that enough of her time and her thoughts were devoted to obligations.

She didn't begrudge that. But it was *enough.*

And having her understanding mirrored in Yugho, she was able to make a decision.

Having made it, she did not have to tell him what it was.

And Yugho, who had chosen to be bound by very little, offered her a second bowl of stew.

*

The house-blessing party commenced at noon with the blessing itself.

Lhennuen had been approached some weeks earlier by the Laupitas' head of house, who had asked her if she would perform the blessing. She had declined. The first time she had been alone with the village priest, Theve Bisyebanto Iste, months past, Lhennuen had looked in his eye and told him: "Uncle, I respect your position in your village. I have no claim to your post or interest in impinging on your duties and rights."

And he had given her a tolerant look that said: *Only someone so young would be so blunt.*

But it was not because Lhennuen was incapable of subtlety that she had chosen to be blunt. Youths are blunt: but so are warriors. And logicians.

She was remembering that promise when she answered Granduncle Laupita's request. But this time, she spoke with subtlety. Or at least, with a politic lie.

"It would be an honor, sir," she said with a bow. "But I am afraid it is one that must be considered. I am not the priest of this place. I have put my blessings upon your house as I worked on it; it has all of my power it can hold. Should it not have its final consecration from someone whose blood is of your people, who has officiated the marriages of your sons and daughters and has blessed your harvests for years past, and, God willing, years to come?"

Granduncle Laupita was a canny man, and he had accepted that as a refusal. It had probably been an offer of courtesy in any event.

So it was Theve Bisyebanto who stiffly cast salt in the home's corners; he who drew the marks of benediction above the doors; he who oversaw the installation of the house gods at their altar by Granduncle Laupita and his sister, the female head of house.

Lhennuen stood at the edge of the crowd. They were all in their finery, as if for a wedding. She smiled and was truly as happy as they were; but she wore her robe over her dress.

*

The feast went well. The Laupitas were not as well-to-do as the

Sasanges, so there was no imported fruit, but there were honeyed cakes and sultry roasts and dishes flavored with spices that had come up the river. The feast was held in the common hall, which was the only building in the village large enough. Lhennuen ate between the head builder and a senior Laupita woman she didn't know well.

After the feast was the party, open to all. The benches were pushed to the walls to clear a dance floor, the doors to the hall were opened, and savories were set out. It was warm enough that the party spilled outside onto the village green. Musicians struck up a tune. The young and the nimble made lines and set to dancing—and laughing, when they got the lines intertwined wrong and the dance ended in a near pile-up.

At this time of year the night lasted only a handful of hours; Lhennuen had not got used to that and she wasn't sure she ever would. But the sun was dipping a little, which meant it was quite late indeed.

She was sitting on the low stone wall along the side of the green, slowly drinking a mug of wine. She was thinking that when the wine was done she would go home and see if Yugho wanted to dance. Her smile was genuine; it was good to be among happy people. Had she been at home—back in Kasith, that was—she would have danced, or played the kanna. But she'd made her choice already.

"Not dancing, Siol?" someone said in passing.

"Hmm! It looks dangerous," she said with a laugh.

"You're right. I've got bruises," said the man ruefully. "I had better medicate myself with some wine."

She chuckled and he went on. He had already been medicating himself quite a bit, it looked like.

Her wine was down to the dregs when Nazu Sasange showed

up.

Lhennuen knew she was coming a moment before she appeared. And in that moment, she considered the gymnastic feat of going over the other side of the wall. But there were a dozen people, either sitting along the wall or milling about with snacks, who would see, and there was too much of a drop on the other side to make it look natural. So in hesitating, Lhennuen lost her chance.

But she did at least have a second to prepare herself. All right—Nazu would do what Nazu would do. But Lhennuen would not give Nazu the pleasure of seeing that she had disturbed her peace. She rested her mug on her lap, loose in one hand, and crossed one leg over the other with an air of insouciance.

Then Nazu was there. Lhennuen looked down at her. The old woman's face was as sour as a pickle.

It had a been a game for her at first, Lhennuen realized: barbs traded with an interloper who refused to be cowed. Then it had been Nazu's own house that came down, and her mistrust had been proven righteous.

Nazu's anger had needed a focal point. And once it had been declared, pride had fixed it like an inkstain.

Nazu was not *all* a fool, but she had a little mind—tight and gnarled, like a dog biting itself raw in pursuit of fleas.

Lhennuen pitied her.

"So you'll be guest of the Laupitas, but not the Sasanges, is that so?" Nazu said, loud enough to cut over the music. "You'll drink my neighbor's wine, but not mine?"

Lhennuen answered in a normal tone—which nevertheless carried well, if you were listening.

Which everyone was, now.

"I've nothing against the Sasanges," she said. "Though I think at least one of them has something against me."

Nazu laughed. "Is that what you think?"

She gave Lhennuen time to answer, but Lhennuen merely looked down at Nazu in silence.

"Well, you're right," Nazu said at last. "I *do* have something against you. No one else will say the truth that needs to be said. They're all so damn polite—you'd think they kissed the asses of the Autransis every evening. But *I'll* say it.

"You're a meddler, girl!

"My family has been of this village for eight generations. It's *our place.* Pardon me, but *we* know what's best for us. You've come and changed our river, which has run in its course for thousands of years! Just because it's with the agreement of the village council doesn't make it right. And you've decided our houses weren't fit to be rebuilt. Even though carpenters said my home was sound enough."

One of her sons-in-law was the (singular) carpenter who had declared this. Someone in the crowd protested, and was shushed. Lhennuen did not look to see who it was.

Nazu used the interruption as an excuse to raise her voice to a near shout.

"Who gave you the authority to decide? You're—what are you, twenty years old? Eighteen? What do you know? What you've read in books? That's not experience. Do you think God gives you the authority to meddle in our lives, because you made some promises to a priesthood? Well, the Gods gave me *my* authority. They gave it to me by blessing me with a long life—as authority should be earned: through experience!

"Do you think that grey robe you wear gives you the authority to decide for us, who are not your people? Brute force isn't authority, either. You simply *haven't the right*.

"So hear this that I say, *Siol*: Go back home. Mind your family's business, as you should. Mind that war you silly southerners are always fighting. Everything you do shows you disdain us: those fancy boughten dresses you wear. Your keeping away from our holiday feasts. Your bizarre boyfriend, who, let's face it, isn't right in the head. Your prissy manners—even worse than the rest of us in not saying what you're really thinking! A sensible person, when insulted, stands up for herself. But you're a cold fish. You think that's a good thing, to have no heat in your blood?

"We're not really good enough for you, are we? Yes, you are right, *Siol* Lhennuen Hegaantendre Damaiud e Kasith, Belim Hadheran. I don't like you. Because I don't like people who don't keep to their own places. And you're very far from your place, miss. *Go back home.*"

Nazu was going to turn away, and let whatever rebuttal Lhennuen chose to make drop into the dust. But Lhennuen saw her begin to move, and used the only magic she would ever use against someone like Nazu Sasange. She spoke: and by speaking, held her to listen.

Or to appear to listen, at least. It was the appearance that was important.

Lhennuen looked into Nazu's eyes.

"You think I should go back to my family, Nazu?" she said. Not loud. Calm. She held up her hand, showing her the mark of circle and triangles on the back. "A millennia or so ago, to become a priest, I would have had to burn away my tattoo—renouncing all claim to my family and their claims upon me. These days I can keep the mark; but it's still true. No matter how long I live, I can never become the head of my house. I might have a bed at the birevo Damaiud, but the only place that I owe duty to now is the ground beneath my feet—wherever that may be. So for today it is not only my right, but my honor, to serve the village of Herede—for which, last I checked, you do not speak."

She added softly: "And if you truly believe that everyone should always keep to their own, then I can only disagree. I think that leads to a small and cramped life. As priests of Vigu say—'If one never walks among strangers, no friends can be made.'"

Nazu was more visibly furious than Lhennuen had ever seen her. This was not the argument she had wanted. Lhennuen thought the thing that maddened her the most was that Lhennuen would not fight; would not even answer Nazu's insults directly.

If Nazu could not understand the reason why now, at her age, she never would.

"Vigu is the goddess of sluts and whores," Nazu Sasange spat.

Lhennuen thought of a rebuttal involving the number of Nazu Sasange's descendants, but she did not say it. Instead she smiled faintly.

"There is no pleasing some people."

Then she sat back and said:

"Was that all? I believe we were in the middle of a party."

Nazu stood and looked at Lhennuen with scorn for a long moment.

"The way you act—it's not even human."

Lhennuen smiled suddenly, with full force. Nazu looked taken aback.

"Then perhaps you should expand your definition," she said.

*

As always with public confrontations it was the moments afterward that were the worst. When Nazu had gone, pushing her way through the crowd, Lhennuen felt a flush on her cheeks and was glad no one could see it in the dying light. Her stomach roiled. But she could control her face. She looked calmly at the partiers who had stopped to watch. And they *were* watching, openly; most of them were a little drunk.

There was the Zhasse head of house, leaning on a cane, his lips thin with controlled anger; Ereshezhu Farogento, behind the crowd, flushed with drink and not hiding his anger at all; a pair of teenage Ketelle twins, clever masons, both agape at witnessing something beyond their experience and sobriety; a little girl with a mass of flyaway blond Seianshe hair, ready to cry. A dozen men and women—their faces in turn confused, angry, afraid, sympathetic. Lhennuen knew them; she knew everyone by now.

And she knew, even before she reached out with her mind and touched the faint waft of emotions in the air, that it was not her they were angry at.

She looked at each of them in the small moment when her power unconsciously reigned over their drunkenness.

This, here, she thought: this is the moment of the actual battle. *What I say to them now is a thousand times more important than what I have said to Nazu.*

There were too many paths before her. To say nothing to them, and let them rant and apologize and opinionize; or to tell them it didn't matter, and risk someone arguing back that it *did*; or to mock Nazu, and risk the wrath of the Sasanges; or to pretend it didn't happen, and have to bear much awkwardness, because it *had*—

She'd been trained for this kind of battle, alongside the kind fought with swords. Yet despite her training, she was afraid she wouldn't find the answer.

At the last possible second, it came. She slid down off the wall.

"Well," she said to them, wryly, "let's all have another round of drinks."

That did it. The anger slipped away, fear relaxed, sympathy relieved. They came around her and touched her arms and made jokes awkward and drunken, to which she smiled and did not respond. Someone fetched her another drink, which she did not want. As she drank it, she wondered if sometimes she was too good at what she had been trained for.

There was her victory over Nazu Sasange, in the war of public opinion; but what a complicated victory it was. She was not sure she had earned it.

*

The music faded and the lanterns dimmed to fireflies behind her as she walked down to the riverside an hour later. She would fly, but she wanted a moment first.

When she came to the new bridge, she stopped, and leaned over the railing to look at the water. A thousand lights of stars sparkled on its black surface. She breathed deeply of the cool night air.

It was an old spell, to stand on a bridge and drop one's cares into the water; but first she had to establish what they were. And she wasn't sure what she was feeling, just then.

But she had time only for a few breaths before she sensed

someone coming down the riverside path. At first, thinking the shadowed figure was passing by, she only turned her head to bid him goodnight. But he stopped on the bridge near her, and she looked closer. She could just make out his face in the moonlight.

It took her a second to remember his name.

"I've come to apologize for my grandma," said Teido Nazunto Sasange. "If you'll let me."

Lhennuen turned fully, and leaned back against the railing. Teido wasn't a day over fifteen and had no business apologizing for his elders. She was amused, but also touched.

"Apology accepted."

"Whoever said that wisdom comes with age never met *her*," he said ruefully.

"It doesn't matter," Lhennuen said, quiet. "I'm not offended by what truth she speaks, and the rest of it's just shooting arrows in the dark."

"She doesn't like you for some reason. She's not usually this bad. I'm sorry...."

"Thankfully, the peace of my soul does not rest on being liked by Nazu Sasange."

She could see him nod. He hesitated for a moment, and she thought he was going to go. But then he surprised her by hopping up to sit on the railing beside her. They faced into the moon, and light was cast across his face. She looked over at him, raising her eyebrows.

"Do you like it here?" he asked.

Lhennuen's brow knitted.

"What do you mean?"

"Do you like coming here every day...to the village?"

She had to think carefully. The moon was too bright, and drew her eyes, so she turned around to look down at the water once more, leaning her elbows on the railing.

"I like to work," she said at last. "I like finding trees, even if it's sad that they'll be felled. I like the accomplishment of building something. I like working with people of skill. I like Aistra Isshainto because he's so—" she sketched her hands in the air, searching for a word.

"Energetic with ideas," Teido supplied.

Lhennuen laughed. "Energetic with ideas. And he's honest. I like Tayitoös-Barema because she interests me. I like Dob Renni. She reminds me of my mother." Lhennuen smiled. "I like your grandmother, believe it or not—she speaks her mind even when everyone else disapproves. That's important. And...I like this conversation."

"You like the interesting and unusual people," Teido said.

She laughed again, softly. "I guess so. Are you unusual?"

"I'm here having this conversation, so I must be," he retorted.

"Well, there you go then."

Teido kicked his legs, but was careful not to knock into the freshly-installed rails.

"I'm sorry you don't like all of it, though," he said. "I think maybe our manners are rougher than you're used to. No civilization for miles out here."

"My last job was with the army guarding the border. I'm quite used to rough manners, I assure you."

"Did you like *that?*" he said.

She considered again, wanting to be honest. "It was very tiring. There was a lot of doing nothing. And then there would be a lot of very hard work for a while. And then a lot more doing nothing."

He nodded thoughtfully, taking that in.

After a minute he said, "We were all kind of wishing you would snap and kick her teeth in. Or at least tell her where to stuff it."

Lhennuen opened her mouth and then closed it. She wasn't sure what to say.

"Didn't you want to?" Teido said.

She hesitated. But she found no answer but to tell the truth. "Sure. Of course I did."

"You should've. Next time, you should. You of all people can do it."

"I won't," she said.

He made a frustrated noise. "Why the hell not?"

"Maybe because...as a Siol, I am entitled to break the rules...so I am more aware of what they are. I have to pick my battles; and no good would come of that one, whether I won or lost."

"But what good is being able to break the rules if you never *do?* She was right about that. You follow the rules *all* the *time*. It does make you kind of stand-offish."

Lhennuen looked over at the side of his face that she could see. "I'm sorry if that disappoints you."

"But you find more interesting people if you break the rules," he protested. "If you're following the rules, you only say what's necessary. But if you throw in some unnecessary stuff, and maybe be a little rude like I am, you get into interesting conversations like this one and that's how you find out, maybe, how everyone is unusual. And then you might like it here better."

Lhennuen looked at the moon on the rippling water, flickering like a white flame. She was silent.

Finally she said: "I came here—here to this province, I mean; I didn't know about Herede at the time—to...rest. Not physically, but mentally. And I don't think I've yet had enough time to do that."

She had almost said "to mourn." But she hadn't told any of the villagers that she'd been widowed, recently or otherwise; they knew only (because they had asked) that she had been married once. And she'd offered no more information, so they probably figured her for a divorcée. It felt dishonest, not to tell Teido now; but she did not want to have to deal with his sympathy or his curiosity.

She said: "I find making friends to be a lot of work—because that's what I think you mean, making friends; because once you have interesting conversations with people, you can start to be their friend. But I'm not sure I want to do that work at the moment."

Teido blew out a breath.

"Well. I think that stinks, because you might be here for a while." He hopped down from the railing. "Just keep in mind...being rude gets easier with practice."

Lhennuen laughed softly.

"I'll keep that in mind. I'll think about it."

Teido shrugged. "All right." He thumped his hand on the railing. "Well, I've got to get back to my girlfriend. She already has a low opinion of me; I don't want to give her any ideas by hanging out with an older woman."

Lhennuen smiled. "Good night, Teido. You more than make up for your grandmother."

"See? That's what I'm talking about. Using first names before I told you it was okay. G'night, Lhennuen."

*

Her conversation with Teido, as much as she had enjoyed it, exhausted the last of Lhennuen's reserves. The next day, she went back to bed after breakfast. She was grateful that the day after a holiday was assumed to be a day of recovery. The Heina frowned on drinking to excess—except during celebrations, when it was nearly mandatory.

It wasn't a hangover she was recovering from, but it might as well have been.

Yugho came to join her after a few hours, and they slept curled up together like wolves in a den.

It was nice to pretend, Lhennuen thought, half-waking just after noon, that she was a thing of the wild, like the wolves and the lynx and even like Yugho.

She went back to sleep.

*

The next day she was ready to work again, and so were the villagers. There was a distinctly odd feeling in the air, which she was at a loss to interpret or even define. Were they being more courteous than usual? Or sillier? And was it due to their being refreshed from the day off; their sense of pride in finishing the second house; or something else? She wondered if she had missed something that had happened after she'd left the party.

Whatever it was, she eventually decided that the change, whatever exactly it was, was for the better. It seemed to have a positive effect on their productivity, at least. They felled a record number of trees that morning.

At lunchtime they scattered in loose groups, chatting and joking as they sought out seats in the patchy grass and on stumps and against tree trunks. Lhennuen found a place under a birch tree.

"Mind if I sit here?" said Dob Renni, patting a mat of moss across from her.

Lhennuen looked up from unwrapping her meat pasty. All her senses went on the alert. "Of course I don't mind. Go ahead."

Dob was a big woman, and getting all the way onto the ground made her grunt. But once she was there, she lotused her legs as elegantly as an Autransi.

"Care for some jerky? It's reindeer. Not bad, if I do say so myself."

Lhennuen leaned forward and availed herself of a strip. "Thank you."

Dob Renni smiled. But it was more than the usual smile she made when humored—it was arch and wicked and very, very amused by something. Lhennuen gnawed on the jerky and eyed her with suspicion.

"So," Dob said, still smiling, "I was talking to a little kitten last night. And that little kitten told me *I remind you of your mother.*"

Every conversation in the vicinity stopped; every ear turned in their direction.

Lhennuen nearly choked.

What had Teido done! What had he said—

And then a second later, she saw why he had done it. He'd decided that she needed friends. So he'd willfully ignored what he was plenty old enough to know—that their conversation had been a private one, not to be spread around as gossip. Even (or especially) if it amused the others.

She couldn't thank him for betraying her confidence, but she understood the reason for it. He'd meant well.

Not that she was not going to box him on the ears next time

she saw him—on principle.

Lhennuen finished chewing and swallowed. She composed herself with every scrap of calmness she could collect.

"You do," she said. "And it's a compliment to you both. Though my mother's not a woodcutter: She's a captain in the army."

And there, she got the better of Dob, because the other woman's eyebrows shot up.

"A *captain?* You're having me on. I know there's a few women in the army, maybe, but we can't be *officers.* What's next, a woman general?"

"My mother," Lhennuen said dryly, "is not greatly a fan of the word 'can't.'"

"I think I like the sound of her," said Dob Renni. "Tell me more...."

*

She didn't actually box Teido on the ears, but she did cuff him soundly on the shoulder.

"OW! Hell!" He jumped back, rubbing the bruise. He eyed her reproachfully. Then something seemed to occur to him. "Wait—how long were you sitting behind that hedge? Were you waiting for me?"

"Yes—because you've been avoiding me. And it didn't take a genius to figure out that you have to walk down this path when you visit your girlfriend after dinner."

His mouth made a horrified O.

"Merciful and loving Vigu! You didn't talk to *her*, did you?"

Lhennuen crossed her arms and smiled with a touch of menace. "No, but I retain the option."

He grimaced, then looked glum. "What do you want?"

"To leave a bruise," Lhennuen said. "Did I succeed?"

He gave her a cock-eyed look as he realized something.

"You're not actually mad," he said in wonderment.

"And you're too smart for your own good," Lhennuen said. "I mean that literally. The only reason I'm not kicking your ass is because I like Dob Renni and I have a sense of irony. Listen, Teido Nazunto! Consider your bruise a warning. You're too old to get away with that kind of thing—*Puaiyi Luvwe*, I became a Siol when I was younger than you! Betray someone's confidence again and you may find yourself in more trouble than you can imagine. You may be smart, but—take this to heart. If you're going to manipulate people you've got to be more subtle about it."

He looked at her, still massaging his shoulder.

"Says someone who knows, eh?" he said at last.

"Everyone manipulates each other," Lhennuen said. "In the words we use, in the looks we give. It's called 'communication.' But as in everything, there are rules as to what you can and you can't do.

"You mustn't think, Teido Nazunto, that I am a rule-follower. I am not. If I were I would not be here. But when you break the rules, you risk alienating people; and if you want to accomplish anything in life, you'll need other people. So any time you break a rule you'd better consider whether it is for a cause worth losing your good name over. Sometimes it will be. Most of the time not."

Teido considered.

"You're right," he conceded.

Lhennuen watched him suspiciously.

"Possibly," he said with a grin, "it would have been worth it if I'd been there to see your face when Dob Renni grilled you about your mother."

Calmly, Lhennuen cuffed him hard on the other shoulder. He yelped and then muffled it.

"Did you repeat anything I said to anyone else?" she asked.

"Yes, I told the biggest gossip in the village that you'd wanted to knock my grandmother's teeth in, but hadn't because you didn't think it was a battle worth fighting."

Lhennuen could not stop herself from laughing, somewhat in horror, somewhat in disbelief, and somewhat because she envied Teido his freedom.

"And I did you a favor," said Teido doggedly, "because they all like you better now."

Lhennuen struggled to stop laughing. "Yes, I would too. Was that it? Please say that was it; I've run out of shoulders to slap."

"That was it! I swear on your lady Hadhera and my lady Vigu."

"I don't think Vigu's going to be your goddess when you've grown up a bit," Lhennuen murmured. But Teido, if he heard, was concerned with something else.

"So you really aren't mad at me," he said, not too sure.

"I am," Lhennuen said. "But I can still laugh. You are bright enough to see that they are not mutually contradictory, I think."

Teido frowned at her for a long moment.

"I hope you've enjoyed this," said Lhennuen, suddenly finding a greater truth on her tongue, "because it's your last triumph of this nature for a while. You're too clever by half, and you mean well, but that can get you in loads of trouble. And people are slower to forgive the clever than the stupid."

She shook her head, abruptly aware of rain coming on. She did not want to foretell Teido's future and she could say nothing more to him that would not be repeating herself.

"Good night, Teido Nazunto Sasange. I wish you luck and skill."

She gave him a Hena court bow, hand to forehead, elegant, not mocking. She had been bested by a Sasange after all.

She turned and walked away.

But she looked back before she turned the corner around the hedge. He was still there, watching her with a creased brow.

"If you decide you want to do something else with your life," she called to him, as the rain started to patter on the hedge and on her hair, "I can see that you get the opportunity. That's the curse I bestow on you—for betraying my confidence."

Then she went.

*

After seeing how drained Tayitoös had been by curing the lumber, Lhennuen had cured the last few batches herself. It was a complicated, tedious spell, but she had more than enough power to fuel it. Now, a week after the Laupitas' house-blessing party, they had enough wood cut for another batch. But when Lhennuen went to the yard they had appropriated to store it, she found the job had been done. Tayitoös was alone, walking up and down among the stacks, inspecting her work. Her gait was as stiff as an old woman.

This time, Lhennuen said: "Tayitoös."

Tayitoös turned. She watched with dulled eyes as Lhennuen approached.

Lhennuen held out her hand.

"I don't know whether if would offend you to ask if you would let this be my task in the future," she said quietly. "Meaning no offense, I ask it. I'll do it from now on unless you object.

"Will you trust me, to take my hand?"

Tayitoös looked at her for a moment without any expression but a slight widening of her eyes.

And then she began to laugh. Low at first, as if it hurt a little; and then she closed her eyes and laughed fully, arms wrapped around her stomach to support her still-tired body. When she straightened, she was smiling crookedly.

"You are so Hena," she said.

"Undoubtedly," Lhennuen said, her hand still extended.

Tayitoös reached out and took it. Lhennuen looked in the other woman's eyes and said a few words; and felt energy go trickling from her hand to Tayitoös's, the power turning from blue to lavender as it passed. Tayitoös shifted her stance with a soft exhalation, her shoulders dropping as the pain went from her body. After a moment the spell was done, and they released their hands.

Tayitoös was grinning. "Thanks, Siol," she said. "You're right, I probably would have been offended. But you asked so nicely, and I'm too tired for pride, so go ahead and have at it."

Lhennuen was taken aback. "You're welcome."

"Come eat lunch with us tomorrow," Tayitoös said, with a high-spirited light in her eyes that Lhennuen was not sure how to interpret. "In the kitchen."

And with that she had gone, stepping lightly, before Lhennuen had a chance to answer.

*

"Just because I invited you into the kitchen," Tayitoös said, peering out the door, "didn't mean you had to come in via the barnyard. But what's done is done. Welcome, by any entrance."

She threw the door wide and Lhennuen came in. She let drop the hem of her skirt which she had been holding out of the muck. She was not sure what to say, other than, "Thank you."

"It is no trouble," Tayitoös said. She used the ordinary, and thus formal, Hena phrase, and it was odd to Lhennuen, because there was still a distinct Tsiani informality about the other woman.

"Come in—sit down over here. It's too warm to be near the fire! Would you like to hang up your robe?"

Lhennuen stood up again and shed her robe, aware of the irony in giving up her mark of duty so unceremoniously, where she had kept it before. But it was indeed too warm. Tayitoös hung the robe on a hook. Lhennuen sat once more, feeling both awkward, and amused by her own awkwardness.

"Ordinarily in this weather I'd eat outside," Tayitoös went on, calmly glancing back over her shoulder while she juggled pots on the stove. "The problem is, I've forbidden everyone the kitchen today so *they're* all outside. Remarkably bad planning on the part of the weather gods."

Lhennuen grinned.

"I am going to be terribly rude right now and ask you how old you are," Tayitoös said.

Lhennuen raised her eyebrows. "That is pretty magnificently rude."

"Yes, but you don't care," Tayitoös said.

"You're right." Lhennuen didn't know off the top of her head so she worked it out. "Just shy of twenty."

"And how long have you been a Siol?"

"Forever," Lhennuen said dryly. "But, strictly speaking, since I was thirteen."

Lhennuen thought to herself that she seemed to be having a lot of odd conversations lately. Only little children spoke this frankly on so little acquaintance. Well—children, and fifteen-year-old Sasanges who clung onto their childhood for dear life.

And Tsiani, apparently.

She found she liked it.

She chose to enter the spirit of the thing and turned the tables by asking a question of her own. "How long have you been a magician?"

"Forever," Tayitoös said. "I mean that in the strict sense: since birth. Funny, isn't it, that a magician two years old can do magic, but a Siol can do nothing until they chose?"

Lhennuen considered, not wanting to offend by a comparison of the relative power of magicians and Siol. Then she said in a neutral voice, "That's probably a good thing."

Tayitoös put the bread on the table among the other dishes she had laid out. She sat down across from Lhennuen.

"I agree. It's a lot more responsibility, being a Siol. Stop being so politic! You have more power than I have in an eyelash and yes, sometimes I'm jealous, and I get frustrated about what I can't do. But it doesn't matter. When I think about your life, I don't want it. I'd never want any life but mine. I have a good home, a good husband, beautiful children and enough skill to ease suffering. I know I wouldn't have made your choice, if I had been born without magic. I don't have that in my character. To devote my life to serving others—"

"It's not about serving," Lhennuen said, without thinking about it. She had been trained in science, and she corrected errors: be it politic or not. "It wasn't that when I chose it and it isn't now. If you try to make it about serving, it falls apart.

Every Siol I've ever known, as far as I can tell, is as selfish as an animal. It's not a desire to serve: you serve because it's your duty and because it gives you something to do with your power. Serving offers you challenges to test yourself.

"I chose to become a Siol because I would have gone mad otherwise. I could feel it under my skin and in the way I thought and in my dreams. Like I was going to burst. I was saving myself, not thinking of anyone else."

Tayitoös looked at her for a moment.

"Isn't this a far better conversation than if we'd danced platitudes for an hour?"

Lhennuen had a piece of bread in her hand but she had not had a single bite yet. She felt a little shaky. But that wasn't necessarily a bad thing.

"It's exhausting," she admitted. "Are all Tsiani conversations like this?"

"No, of course not. But things move quicker."

Lhennuen shook her head and laughed. "You are the second person in a week to tell me that."

"About Tsiani?"

"No, about conversations. About the necessity of being impolite."

"Well, you said it yourself—'If one never walks among strangers, no friends can be made.' Except it should be, 'if one never *talks* among strangers....'" Tayitoös shrugged and dipped her bread in a dish of chicken with spiced sauce.

"I'd think it would be fairly obvious that I'm not here to make friends," Lhennuen said quietly.

Tayitoös raised her eyebrows a fraction, snorted, and popped the bread into her mouth, looking across the table at Lhennuen as she chewed. Lhennuen had to wait for her response, so she began to eat as well.

"Yes, it's obvious," Tayitoös said at last. "But only in retrospect—now that you tell me. I didn't know you were doing it on purpose. You do a good job, walking that line: Liked and respected but never loved. You do so good a job it seems like it was our own idea—which I suppose is the point. I congratulate you. It's not a line I'd walk, because it's a very narrow one and I'd think it'd be exhausting to balance on. But you seem to have the knack for it."

"I find walking that line, as you put it, easier than having conversations like this with everyone," Lhennuen said.

Then, suddenly aggrieved, she frowned. She looked down to spoon greens onto her plate.

"What's made you mad?" Tayitoös said.

"HA!" Lhennuen said. She ate a bite of chicken in three rapid chews. "I'm not mad at you—I'm mad at God. It's beating me over the head with something I don't care for at all. And using my own damn words to boot! It's very irritating."

Tayitoös was taken aback. She searched for words for a moment.

"Do priests actually talk to gods, then? I mean...."

Lhennuen grimaced. "Oh, let's not get into theology, please! I mean the thing that sends coincidences. The thing that has an opinion about the way you ought to be. God. Either you know what I mean or you don't."

"All right...." Tayitoös said. Her eyes were a little wide. "I do know."

"Well, *that*, then," Lhennuen said with disgust. "It's teaching me a lesson. And I listen to it—I can't not listen. That's one part of being a Siol you can be glad you've missed out on—Tayitoös. Oh, I was wrong a minute ago when I said being a Siol wasn't about serving. It is. But it's not *people* you serve, or any set of ethics. It's about figuring out what the sender-of-coincidences wants from you—and doing it. Whether you want to or not. *Especially* when you don't want to."

"And what does the sender-of-coincidences want from you?"

"To step out of line—apparently." She grimaced again and slopped up some sauce with a piece of bread.

"Hmm. This is delicious. Can I have the recipe?"

*

Lhennuen did nothing in specific differently. That was not how it worked. She had a long acquaintance with both herself and God, and she knew that It did not want her to be anything but herself. But she knew that at some moment she would know to make a different decision than she would have before; and she would do it; and things would be better than they would have otherwise.

"Better," of course, according to God. It and Lhennuen had disagreed on some occasions.

She did agree that it was *better*, when she made a joke to Dob Renni that made the woodcutter laugh so hard she had to sit down on a felled log and gasp for breath. Having caused delight, Lhennuen was happy all the rest of the day.

And it was better, when in the week before the next house-blessing party, she hailed one of the carpenters, who belonged to family Opei, and asked, without beating around the bush, about the loan of their kanna. It turned out that the instrument was gathering dust in an attic and they were delighted to see it played. The next day, two strong young Opeis delivered it to the common hall, where she could come and go to practice whenever she liked.

Yes, yes, you're right, she said to God. You're always right. Now go gloat somewhere else and let me work.

*

Time passed in ordinary ways. Midsummer came, and the villagers complained of the heat. Lhennuen shook her head and smiled. Tayitoös, from the far south, laughed uproariously. Finally, when it got hotter and the gardens had to be watered twice a day, even Tayitoös admitted that it was a little warm.

Tayitoös had given Lhennuen a standing invitation to lunch at Soskulus birevo. When Lhennuen was working in the forest it was impossible to go, but even when she was in the village with the builders, she did not often take Tayitoös up on the offer. Lhennuen thought that she might like to be friends with Tayitoös, but in a stroke of irony, it seemed to be impossible to get her alone. For at midday when the workers lunched, so did everyone else. The kitchen of Soskulus birevo was taken over by the whole family, from babes in arms to teenagers to the heads of house, and also the Ketelles whom the Soskuluses had taken in until their home was rebuilt. Lhennuen had had introductions but was still not sure how many there were altogether and who belonged to which house.

It was a nice thing to visit now and then and have something warm to eat, but Lhennuen had never found the company of small children to be entirely satisfactory. And it was with them, and with the food, that Tayitoös naturally had to occupy herself. So most days Lhennuen ate a packed lunch at the construction site, either alone or with whomever was avoiding their own family.

On one day, however, when she had joined the Soskulus clan, Tayitoös stubbed her toe on a log as she was checking the stove.

"*Tsusi!*" she swore in Tsiane.

The little girl who was sitting on Lhennuen's lap looked around with big eyes. "Are you okay, mommy?"

Tayitoös hopped around, sputtering. "*Yos saonre!* No, I've broken my toe," which was an exaggeration. "WHO PUT THAT LOG THERE?"

"You did," said one of Hoei's sisters. "And watch your language."

Watch your language. That got Lhennuen thinking.

It turned out that she had lied to Aistra Isshainto after all, all those months ago: there *was* something she wanted. That night after eating dinner with Yugho she flew back to the village to ask.

Tayitoös laughed at first, disbelieving.

Then she looked at Lhennuen for a long while, who sat before her in the Soskulus kitchen with her hands folded in her lap, her face frozen to hide her excitement. Tayitoös's disbelief vanished.

"Why? Why do you want to learn the language of the people who are your enemies?"

Lhennuen blinked. That had not occurred to her.

Her family and friends fought the Tsiani every day, but she had forgotten. Tayitoös had not.

"At first, just for the knowledge," Lhennuen said at last. "But later, I hope, for friendship."

Tayitoös's olive skin darkened with a blush. She said, "Ha," and got up and poked at the stove.

Her answer was addressed to the pot that held the sourdough.

"Well—get yourself some books. And come back again tomorrow evening, if that suits you."

*

Lhennuen had never set out to learn another language before, as strange as that was. Of course she spoke Hadra as well as Henanue, but she could not remember a time when she had not understood both. Henanue was just a worn-down version of Hadra in any event, like a rock that had been polished to smoothness by time. The underlying mineral was the same.

Naturally, she couldn't help but know a few dozen words and phrases of Tsiane already—greetings, curses, trader's terms, the names for troop movements. She found memorizing vocabulary easy and was soon able to name everything in the kitchen and in the women's workroom. But when she tried to put words into phrases she got tangled up. What business had a verb being anywhere but at the beginning of a sentence? And the nouns did *what* with themselves?

The language didn't even have an "L" sound in most dialects —so if Lhennuen had been born Tsiani she would have been "Renuan": and stress on the middle syllable, not the first. It was painful to her ears almost to the point of insult.

Tayitoös was a demanding teacher. She made Lhennuen practice everything time and time again, until Tayitoös approved that her accent and intonation sounded *almost* native. Then she redoubled her attack on syntax. She would let no awkwardness pass uncorrected.

"Because you speak well in Henanue," she said, when Lhennuen complained that it hardly mattered. "You have to learn to speak with equal elegance in Tsiane, or you'll feel like a child. That's why I won't let it go."

Lhennuen realized belatedly that learning a language was not like learning history or science. Those you could read over, once for understanding, twice for remembering, and you could consider it learned.

No, this was like learning to fight. Intellectual understanding served little good. Fighting and speaking: they were feats of the body, not the brain. Nothing but hours of practice would etch the right movements into your muscles, the right instincts into your tongue.

It was grueling. And Lhennuen, who had not been challenged by much in her life, loved it.

"*Yesterday I went to the river.*"

"*Today I went to the river.*"

"*Today I am going to the river.*"

"*Today I will go to the river.*"

"*Tomorrow I will go to the river.*"

"*Yesterday I helped cut trees*—fell *trees. Today I lifted lumber. Tomorrow I will probably do the same thing. Last year I served with the army. This year I'm helping building houses.* To build *houses. Next year*—" Lhennuen broke off with a wry smile. "Who knows?"

"Say it in Tsiane. *Vis gakavise.* 'Who knows?' Keep going."

In between drill sessions, they found time to become friends. Lhennuen was fascinated by Tayitoös's tales of her Tsiani life; Tayitoös in turn found Lhennuen's childhood barely credible and her training as a priestess bizarre. ("Your mother is *what*? And you studied *what*?") The other women of the house drifted in and out of the workroom, joining in the conversations at first, but soon enough Tayitoös insisted Lhennuen speak Tsiane as much as possible, and Tayitoös's adopted sisters and aunts and their Ketelle guests rolled their eyes and left the two odd ones to their own business.

They argued about religion, compared notes on the differences between their magics, and did what women always do and laughed riotously about men. Tayitoös mocked Lhennuen's impatience with needlework and her antipathy towards babies (invariably mutual) but could not deny her skill at spinning a fine and even yarn while reciting the conjugations of irregular verbs.

After a while, Lhennuen realized that one of the subtle things she liked most about Tayitoös was that Tayitoös unquestioningly accepted how, every evening, Lhennuen would fly home to eat dinner with Yugho, then fly back to the village for an hour or two of language lessons and a bit of practice on the kanna, before flying home again once more.

A less astute friend might have pointed out that Gating would have been enormously faster than flying. Or that staying for dinner would save a lot of time. Tayitoös never did.

And a less astute friend would have encouraged Lhennuen to visit on the holidays, instead of matter-of-factly inquiring, afterward, if she'd read anything of interest on her day off, or had any interesting conversations in the forest. With God, or the grouse, or her lover.

It was because those were the kinds of questions Tayitoös asked that she was indeed Lhennuen's friend.

*

Though one conversation Lhennuen had with Yugho was between them alone.

She had come home hours before from her language lesson.

It was very late and the outside world was unreal; all that existed for them was each other, facing one another as they lay on the bedmat. In order to talk, they needed space between them for the flicker of his hands; but their bare feet curled together under the blanket. There was just enough light from the burning-down fire that she could see his hands, and his expressive face.

Tonight they were discussing religion. She knew already that Yugho took a dim view of it, an opinion conveyed shortly after they'd met with a shrug of the hand and a half-smile. Not that he objected to the Gods; it was merely that his world was so full it did not require them. Of the priesthood his objection was more concrete, but she was not offended. He disliked anything organized.

But he surprised her, in the middle of this conversation, by saying that he sometimes stood in the forest and found that he had to express praise and awe at its beauty to something greater than himself, but smaller than the Eternal.

In that case, he said, *I speak to Vigu.*

Lhennuen laughed in surprise. Vigu was the goddess of beauty, yes; but also of romantic love, the most human of all human things. Not a goddess she would immediately associate with Yugho.

"Vigu—not Holu?"

Yugho frowned. *Holu is no longer the god of nature alone, ibut also the god of tricks. There's a meanness in him, which humans have given him, unfairly. Nature doesn't have that. But Vigu is still pure.*

Lhennuen nodded. She hadn't thought of it that way.

"I also have a fondness for Vigu," she said. "I—"

And she stopped. She had almost begun a story without considering whether she wanted to tell it.

She carefully tested inside her mind whether she wanted to

tell the story; whether she wanted to tell it to Yugho; whether she wanted to tell it now.

"I met Davrith at the temple of Ves Vigu in Avven," she said at last.

Yugho raised an eyebrow. He was reacting not with surprise, to the fact of her choosing to tell him this particular story now—he accepted that instantly—but with humor, to the idea of Lhennuen meeting her husband in the temple of the holy prostitutes.

"Yes, I know," she said, smiling a little. "I was fifteen, barely. I was a novitiate, doing my week's temple duty there before I could be confirmed as a full priestess."

His other eyebrow went up. His mouth quirked. His hands didn't move, but he was making fun of her. And what did Vigu's temple duty entail, exactly?

She had to laugh.

"You have a dirty mind," she said. "But no, they kept us—me and the three other visiting novitiate girls—well away from the temple visitors. The other girls were very disappointed by that; I think they had been expecting fancy dress parties and the opportunity to act like profligates. We studied aesthetics, art, diplomacy, fashion, psychology, conversation, social refinements. Twelve hours a day. It was all very practical, and I was enjoying it. ...Except for the class on cosmetics. I suspect I flunked that one, though I was never absolutely sure; the teacher was too diplomatic to throw me out."

He was laughing now, silently.

"On the fifth day they judged us fit to be seen briefly at a private party. We had *strict* instructions to do our jobs and then let the more experienced priestesses handle things. I was to offer the handwashing bowl at the entrance—a giant silver-plate thing, two feet across—which was considered the worst job because it was enormously heavy, and you didn't have very long to flirt with anyone, unlike the table servers. But I had strong wrists from swordfighting, and I had no interest in flirting, so it suited me."

She had been telling the story as if it was amusing—which it was, in parts—but her ability to go on that way vanished. She paused, found her voice again, and continued evenly.

"The party was a bunch of recent Army recruits who were stationed in the capital while awaiting their first assignments. The other girls thought this was very exciting, but I had no interest in soldiers. I had done a stint of border patrol already. I knew better.

"Davrith was the second man to come in. He was sixteen at the time."

Yugho wasn't laughing any more; he was just looking at her. His sympathy, in anticipation of the end, made it harder to go on than she'd expected. She stopped.

She hadn't thought this through fully. She didn't even know what to tell him.

"There is a running joke in my family that Hegaantendre women all like black-haired men," she said after a while. "Maybe that's what caught my eye."

She closed her eyes for a second. There were so many things she could never express. His voice, his crooked half-smile, the little white scar on his chin, the strength in his hands, the intensity of his laugh. She wished that he *had* left her, as Nazu Sasange had said, instead of ceasing to exist. At least that way she would know that somewhere in the world, he was finding something to laugh about, despite the absurdity of life.

She opened her eyes and resumed. This next bit was a good part of the memory.

"When my job was done, I went and sat near the wall. I tried to listen to the way the senior priestesses controlled the conversation to keep everyone comfortable, but Davrith had a lovely voice that I could pick out of the crowd. The man across from him was making a preposterous argument, and Davrith was quietly ripping apart his logic."

Yugho's hand flickered. *Of course you would...* and she could finish the sentence: *fall for a man while he was arguing a point of logic.* She smiled slightly.

"After a bit, he noticed me looking at him. I was very embarrassed but not sorry. He came and sat next to me.

"I was wearing Vigu's gold and orange gowns and had my hair done up ridiculously, but he still said, 'You don't belong here.'

"I said I was a novitiate of Hadhera, not Vigu. So if he wanted to get laid that night he had better keep looking; but he was welcome to stay otherwise.

"He stayed."

There were certain conversations that could not be repeated. She jumped over it.

"We went out to sit in the garden and talked for hours. He told me he wanted to court me, even if it had to be by letter. But...he told me that he knew he would not live to be twenty-one. And he wouldn't court me unless I knew it also.

"When I said I wanted him to anyway, he took my hand and kissed it. He was so happy...and I was ready to cry.

"I didn't cry then, because I didn't want to spoil the time we had together; but after one of his friends came to collect him before their curfew, I did. All night."

She had reached the original point of her story: why she loved Vigu.

"The priestess in charge of us novitiates was named Maro. She was around fifty years old, I think, but still the most beautiful woman I have ever seen. She was Vigu incarnate, inside and out. Beautiful, graceful, kind—and as smart as a raven.

"She gave me my assignment the next day: greeting guests again. I had got out of bed and washed my face and put on the pretty clothes, but I was—I was barely functional. I felt that at that moment the duty of being pleasant to strangers was actually worse than being shredded by razors. At least if you were being tortured, you could honestly scream. I screwed up my courage and said I wasn't feeling up to it; could I please do something else?

"Maro gave me a job in the perfumery, but I should have known I couldn't pull anything over on her. After ten minutes she called me to her office.

"She had a half-dozen floor-pillows in her office—all slip-covered to be easily washable, of course—" Yugho grinned "—but she didn't tell me to sit down.

"You have to understand that so far Maro had seemed to like me; or, I think she found me amusing: I was extremely good at saying 'Yes, ma'am' in a variety of ways. But now she looked me over very seriously. I hoped that whatever she had to say she was going to say it quickly, because all I wanted was to curl up in the corner and not move."

"'Lhennuen,' she said, 'you served eight months with the border guard, did you not?'

"Thank the gods, something easy to answer. I said, 'Yes, ma'am.'

"She said, 'I've never been on border patrol, but I've known a few soldiers in my time. Correct me if I'm wrong, but it's my guess that you lived with bad food, uncomfortable cots, leaky tents, long hours, unremitting mental exhaustion, idiotic superiors, and the constant threat of death to you and your friends. And, because you are a young woman, a great deal of unwanted attention from your comrades.'

"I had no idea where this was going. All I could do was answer accurately.

"'Not after the second day, ma'am,' I said. 'And my commanding officer wasn't bad.'"

Yugho laughed, but his face was unbearably sad. Lhennuen could relate the story in a steady voice but not if she looked at him; it was too much to take. Her eyes were fixed on his collarbone.

"Maro gave me a look—and there's nothing like being given a look by the most beautiful woman you've ever met. I said quickly: 'Yes, ma'am, that's essentially true.'

"'I have been to the temple of Hadhera many times,' she said; 'for the first time, when I was doing my own novitiate training. I remember it as a giant stone place a thousand miles from anywhere, with nothing in sight but mud and mountains, not a tree nor growing thing to be found, no animals, thin air, and only scant bits of wood and coal and endless miles of door runners to keep away the roaring drafts. When I was there, I spent most of my time in the basement where I was expected to read, memorize and analyze upwards of six pages a day of text on religion and science. Sometimes they didn't give me a lamp, so I had to read by witchlight, curled up under a pile of furs and still having to do a spell to keep warm. You have had more than a year's training there. Has it changed?'

"'I think they were hazing you with the lamp, ma'am,' I said. 'They always gave us lamps.'

"She sort of frowned.

"'Well,' she said. 'Last month you did your week's duty with the priests of Baros.'

"I think I cringed. Until that morning, it had been the worst week of my life. I could only imagine what it had been like for her as a priestess of Vigu.

"'Of which the less said the better,' she added.

"I didn't really trust myself to answer, so I nodded.

"'In all of this,' she said, 'when assigned a duty, have you ever before said "I don't feel up for it"?'

"I got where she was going now. I almost wished I could lie to her and say that I called in sick all the time. But I managed to say:

"'No, ma'am.'

"'So,' she said, 'why did you say it today?'

"I started bawling, but it was more out of relief than anything.

"'Because I think I've met the man I'm going to marry,' I said, 'and he's only going to live four years.'

"Maro looked surprised, then horrified. She didn't say anything right away.

"'You know Vigu is the goddess of heartbreak, as well as joy,' she said at last; 'but I think you've got them in the wrong order, sweetheart.'

"'I should be grateful I have four years,' I told Maro, 'since my mother only had two with my father, and she didn't have any warning before he died.'

"And Maro said: 'I don't think you are the lucky one'; and she put her arms around me, and cried even harder than I did."

Her voice went, finally, but she managed to scrape out:

"Maro is the reason I love Vigu.

"I spent the next six months weeping and then three years

happy. The six months after that—I don't even know. I still don't know."

Yugho reached for her. Nothing to say.

She was embarrassed for days; telling the story had felt like making an excuse, or asking for sympathy. Eventually she realized that Yugho knew better.

*

The weather turned cooler, to everyone's relief, though it still kept dry. One evening Lhennuen showed up for her language lesson and was told (not so much as asked) that she would be carving turnip lanterns for the next day's harvest festival. It was going to be an enormous feast, as they were combining it with the blessing ceremony of the house that had been completed three days before.

"If you're good with a sword, I'm sure you're good with a knife, too," Tayitoös said.

She didn't even bother looking innocent about "forgetting" to warn Lhennuen about the change of plans. Her face was red from being over the stove, her arms were coated in dough up to the elbows, and she had a toddler clinging to one leg. She returned to filling pasties alongside her sisters-in-law. The Ketelles had since moved out, but given the number of people crammed into the room, you could hardly tell.

Several children of various ages were at the table merrily checking the sharpness of their chosen knives. Lhennuen scooted a child out of the way and sat, amused. Hoei, along with one of his brothers-in-law and the Solau man who was courting one of his sisters all heaved baskets of turnips up onto the long kitchen table. One of the baskets was overturned, the vegetables rolled out, and Lhennuen's jaw dropped.

"*Puaiyi Luvwe!* Those are the biggest turnips I've ever seen in my life!"

One of the little boys giggled and lifted up one of the vegetables with difficulty to demonstrate that it was only marginally smaller than his head.

"You've got that right," Hoei said, pleased by her reaction. "It's been a bumper crop this year. You're our good luck charm, Siol."

Lhennuen smiled, but also snorted. "It must have been the flood. That's always good for the soil."

"Nah, these came from up-slope. It's not just the plain that's growing like crazy—it's everywhere. We've got carrots the size of my arm! And not a rotten veg in sight."

"The size of your *arm?*" she protested, disbelieving. Hoei's arms were nothing to sneeze at.

Hoei's brother-in-law nodded. "He speaks the truth. In this, if in little else."

"Hell, that's nothing," said the would-be brother-in-law cheerily; "*our* carrots were the size of my *dick.*"

The object of his affection, who was on the other side of the table making pasties, burst out laughing.

"You *wish!*"

Lhennuen took one of the giant turnips and turned it over in her hands, trying to decide what carving pattern would best suit its individual bumps and warts. But, always curious about why things were the way they were, she sent out a fragment of her mind to examine the turnip from the inside. Vegetables did not suddenly decide to grow to enormous sizes without a reason, and if she could figure out what it was, the knowledge might be useful someday. Had it just been the hot summer?

Then she was so surprised by what she found in the turnip that she almost dropped it.

It had, indeed, been her doing. Just as Hoei had said. There, woven deep within the twists of unseeable energies that added up, layer upon layer, to a vegetable, were glimmering blue flashes of her own magic.

She knew instantly how it had happened. A memory rose, and she relived a moment she had long forgotten: standing in the woods on a cold winter's night; raising her hands to see a splash of blue light in the sky. Saying: *Use it how You will.*

Until now, she hadn't known what purpose God had decided upon for her gift. Had assumed at the time that she would never know. Now she had discovered, purely by accident, and she wanted to laugh. Both because she was delighted—and because it was funny.

She grinned to herself and dug her knife into the vegetable. She would carve the traditional design, she decided, of a fat serpent around the equator.

But she would put wings on it: A dragon.

Her own little joke.

*

Lhennuen spent the morning of the harvest holiday in bed with Yugho, celebrating. Finally when it was nearly noon she dragged herself up with a yawn and pulled on her dress. She couldn't say why she was so loathe to go out. Yesterday, when carving turnips with the Soskuluses, she had been looking forward to the celebration, but somewhere in the night the idea had soured. She felt unsettled for no defined reason and, because of that, grumpy.

"I don't want to go today," she grumbled to him, "and if it wasn't the damn house-blessing too, I wouldn't. I'd much rather stay with you."

Yugho, still in bed, shrugged his narrow naked shoulders which peeked out from under the ragged blanket.

"Sure you won't come with me?" Lhennuen asked. "I bet you're just as good a dancer on two feet as you are on the wing."

She hadn't asked again since that first time. But there was no reason why not.

He grimaced. Then, after thinking for a second, he flicked a hand in a way that said: *Next time.*

She was surprised, but pleased. "Oh, really?" She sat on her heels beside him. He gazed back at her with sleepy equanimity, like a cat. Despite her pleasure at his promise, she had to say, softly: "It'll be the last one, you know."

He knew, but he made no response, via expression or gesture or even the fragment of a thought in her mind. He only looked at her, steadily.

This was the sixth house built—out of seven. Neither of them knew what she was going to do when the building was done. She would not stay forever: and he would not go.

Lhennuen had been looking for a solution to that for some months now. Yugho, she knew, had not. He did not try to solve things. He had, perhaps, more faith than she did.

He raised his hand in a little gesture of beckoning. She smiled, shifted her position, and leaned down to kiss him.

"You know I'll probably be back late," she said.

He grinned and said with quick sharp movements of his fingers: *I insist that you have fun.* And he touched his heart.

She grinned back. "Your wish is my command. I love you too."

*

She followed his instruction to the letter. She ate far too much, drank more than she usually did, and happily participated as a member of the noisy audience when Theve Bisyebanto first blessed the house and then the harvest. It had indeed been a bumper crop despite the dry weather. Then she danced a couple of turns, chatted with Aistra Isshainto, amused Teido Nazunto to no end by sticking out her tongue at his grandmother's back when no one else was watching, and oohed and aahed with everyone else when the beautifully-carved turnip lanterns were lit at dusk. By popular opinion the best was the work of a young Lotepadh, who had inscribed his turnip with an entire verse from the *Melandis Atha* in exquisite calligraphy.

Then it was time for the serious dancing to begin. Lhennuen had another drink before settling down to play the kanna.

She had played at the last three house-blessing parties. Her fellow musicians were a Solau with a flute, an Opei straddling a wooden box drum, and Ereshezhu Farogento, who, surprisingly for his rough exterior, could coax beautiful things from a lute. They didn't practice together often enough, but the songs were all as old as the forest, so they couldn't go far wrong.

They took their seats near the fire that roared in the hall's huge fireplace. The villagers found themselves partners and shuffled into lines on the dance floor.

Lhennuen felt terribly happy. She loved the heavy, old, gleaming curve of the kanna leaning against her knees and the way its long neck rested in the crook of her own neck like the sweet embrace of a lover. She loved the coarse scrape of rosin on horsehair as she prepared her bow, and she loved the low vibrating plunk the strings made under her fingers as she and Ereshezhu and the flautist swapped notes back and forth in an attempt to get their instruments to agree. At last a consensus was reached. The drummer started off with a warning rattle. Lhennuen played one long note. The flute came in two octaves higher, Ereshezhu strummed a chord and then everyone was off at a madcap pace. The music could barely be heard over the stomp of the dancers' feet and the clap of their hands, but it hardly mattered. They were Hena; these songs were in their blood.

*

They had been playing off and on for a few hours and were in the middle of a particularly sprightly tune when Lhennuen discovered that she was crying.

She kept her head down and let her hair, sprung free from its braid, hide her face. She was sweating from exertion and from the heat of the fire, but her heart seemed to have frozen solid in her chest. She couldn't breathe. When her vision dimmed she forced herself to inhale once, then every four bars, harsh gasps that made her heart ache. Beneath the shield of her hair a tear dropped onto the polished body of the kanna. She watched it roll away, disbelieving.

She had passed over the moment of discovery directly to reaction. Knowledge of something just happened, at a far distance, had come to her so softly she had missed its coming; like the realization, on moment of death, that the drink one has downed is poison. She could not accept what she knew; could not believe it; would not think about it.

Not again, was all she could think, a single thin bitter prayer.

again not again. Not him too. *How could You.*

Yet still her fingers played on of their own volition—driving on the blood in her veins in the rapid rhythm of the notes she plucked. Her hand lifted the bow again and entered the melody on exactly the right beat. Stopping was impossible. The song was a prison of automatic movement from which she could not free herself. It stretched on before her infinitely. Yet at the same time, she dreaded the second that would come after the song ended, and she *was* free. Then she would have to think about why she was crying.

The last note was hers. Of course it was. She had anticipated it, anticipated it, and then not expected it until it came upon her. She realized it had come only when the other instruments fell silent. The trembling of her fingers made a perfect vibrato. She drew out the low note across the whole length of her bow until it was merely a hum felt rather than heard.

Then she was released.

With a swift movement she wiped her hair out of her face, taking sweat and tears of panic with it. She stood, turning away from the other musicians. She leaned the kanna between the chair and the wall and set the bow across the seat. Her mind, like her face, was blank.

She heard the drummer say something behind her as she pushed through the crowd towards the door, but she didn't have the strength to say even "excuse me."

She wanted more than anything in the world to be able tell herself that her Sight was wrong. But it never was.

It was, after all a gift from God.

*

She had left her sword somewhere in the village and now her fingers burned like ice from having cut open the Gate home with her bare hand. She didn't notice the pain.

Her Gate had given her into darkness. The cabin and the trees cut black shapes against the stars above her, but she didn't wait for her eyes to adjust. She sent up a blazing witchlight that made the clearing as bright as day under a blue sun. Owls shrieked curses at her from the trees. She ran the two strides to the door of the cabin and yanked it open. Yet she knew exactly what she would find there; had known even before she'd opened the Gate.

Nothing.

She stood in the doorway to the cabin and looked at the rumpled but obviously unoccupied bedmat. An eerie glow of blue light blazed in through the windows and the door, showing that there was no place for a man to be hidden. For a moment again she forgot how to breathe. All of her body seized: heart, lungs, legs, mind. She clung to the door.

She hadn't even bothered to hope she had been wrong. But some part of her must have, somewhere. Or else why had she come here to look for him?

After a moment she forced herself to live again. Her tears were cold on her face but no more joined them. She went back outside without bothering to close the door. She turned in a circle.

West-southwest.

She threw herself into the sky, shifting and bending air with more than feathers. She canted up over the trees and hit top airspeed within seconds, the canopy flashing by beneath her now seen as if in broad day.

Her forgotten witchlight, hovering over the clearing, went

out abruptly when she was more than a mile away.

*

The wildfire had blackened the forest from horizon to horizon. There was just enough of her mind within the hawk that she could hold that one cramped blank thought: How could You do this?

Again.

The destruction stretched too far for her to see its distant limits even from high in the air. But beneath her she could see that the fire had been snuffed out in the space of one inch to the next as if it had run into an invisible wall and been able to burn no farther. She knew that if she followed the edge around, she would find trees and bushes with leaves fresh and alive on one side—shriveled and black on the other.

Yugho had extinguished the fire so thoroughly that no heat lingered, nor smoke rose.

It was only when she alighted gently in the dry but living moss beside his body, and took back her own form, that she was able to smell the faint scent of char and ash lifted up by the breeze.

She couldn't look at him yet—not even as a faint shape in the dark. She kept her face turned away.

She raised a witchlight, this one more controlled than the last, and sent it a hundred feet into the sky. She looked south into a charred forest of spruce and pine and birch, their skeleton trunks flat and unreal shadows beneath the too-bright, too-blue sun.

It took all of her effort to continue breathing. Anything so complex as *feeling* was impossible.

Thinking, of course, came all too easily.

She didn't understand why Yugho had done it, at first. And that was a small confusion, something she could focus on and sort out, while the larger confusion loomed over everything, untouchable.

Why had he done it? Why had he given himself—for this? The forests were supposed to burn. Every century or so, in a long patient cycle of their own. They depended on it. New life would rise from the ash. Yugho had understood the world he lived in enough to know that.

However much it would have grieved him to let it happen—to see green turn black, to see bears panting in the smoke until they smothered, to see hares and foxes cry and burn in their burrows—he *would* have let it happen. It was supposed to.

But he had not. He had stopped it. And she didn't understand.

She closed her eyes and sent her mind out, stretching recklessly, miles and miles to encompass the burned area. As Yugho had done. She, now, seeking the reason he had.

And then—she knew why.

Though this looked like the depths of the wild, the river Asoi was not twenty miles south. And along it, hundreds of towns, as fragile as paper.

The townsfolk *might* have had their own Siol to protect them. Their own Siol, who was willing to give up every last scrap of his power—his breath, his life—to stop the inferno before it turned their homes to husks in the course of minutes.

Or, perhaps, they had just had Yugho.

Lhennuen ached as if every fragment of her body had been beaten.

"Is that why you feared humanity, Yugho?" she said into the

devastation. "Because you knew you'd end up dying for us no matter how you tried to keep away? Did you foresee it?"

Her words fell into silence. She would never have an answer.

Finally, she looked down at him.

He had no injury on him. He had died. Only that. Fallen where he stood in the moss, his heart stopping, his limbs going limp. In death his face looked young, and soft with innocence. She looked at him and remembered the touch of his hand in her hair that morning.

Yugho the mystery. Yugho, the thing of the wild.

She had always wondered why he had chosen to wear the robe that marked him to others' eyes as a Siol, when he had otherwise turned his back on humanity. Now she understood, a little. The robe had been a recognition that whatever he might wish, he was still bound. That his life was not his own.

Had not been his own.

Of all the questions she had ever had about Yugho—she wished, more than anything, that that one had been answered in any other way. Or left unanswered, if it meant he could have lived.

No longer able to stand, Lhennuen sat down beside his body. With a tug of thought she put out the witchlight. Night fell. Her eyes adjusted. The stars glimmered above her, so many visible through the trees that would normally have blocked her view.

She wrapped her arms around her knees and buried her head in her skirts. The tears she had deferred took away her breath in sobs.

Yugho, she knew, must have been satisfied with the decision he had made, or else he would not have made it. And so it was not for his soul that she wept, but for the rest of the universe, which would no longer witness his beauty.

She did not think there would ever come a time to stop grieving that.

After she was too exhausted to sob any more, she came to weep quietly, but no less intensely, over her own lack of understanding about the desires of God.

Far off, an owl called, commentary on the fine mice rousted by the fire. She raised her head and listened. Then she sat still, looking at the stars through the skeletons of the trees.

"I could have done it," she told the night after a while, her voice thick. "Easily. And I wouldn't have died from it. Why wouldn't You let me do it? You've given me the power; let me use it. Am I a curse to men, that they die doing something I could have done, when I was not there? If that's so, I'll give up loving."

That's got nothing to do with you, said God firmly. They had their own fates.

"Well, when You do it twice," she said with bitterness, "what am I to think? Either that You are random, or that You are cruel. And in either case, why should I continue to serve You?"

The answer came promptly.

It's not necessary for you to know what your purpose was in the lives of these men, God said. As for what purpose they had in yours: Well, you know what Davrith taught you. He taught you what was the pain of love, and with that, educated you in what it meant to be human. But it was not his path to live, and it was not yours to stay in that pattern of life. You touched and parted. Nothing was extra. No energy was wasted.

God seemed pleased with Itself at this. Lhennuen closed her eyes and dug her fingernails into her palm.

"And Yugho? What is this lesson I'm learning from him? From his death? I've been looking, and I've found parts of it, but not the whole."

Because finding the whole of it was not possible until now.

"*What?*" she cried, rocking back and forth. "Tell me, for crying out loud."

Why have you been given this power? Much more—let's be honest—than your contemporaries.

"That's my question, which I've been asking—over and over."

And you've been looking for what great work you can use it on: a thousand troops saved, or killed, the breaking of a dam averted, the unraveling of a universe reknitted...a big flash, that releases all that stopped-up light. And probably ends your life as well.

Lhennuen raised her head and stopped rocking. "I've certainly no desire whatsoever to die. I would hope that I can serve You better than by dying."

Well, said God, pleased, there's your answer, isn't it?

Lhennuen thought about it. Far off, there was the suggestion of light.

"What do you mean?"

Did it never occur to you that I might give you this power so that you would live? So that you would not need to burn out your life to change some slight event like a forest fire or the turn of a battle? So that you could master those things, and go on and do something larger, and far more difficult, by living?

Lhennuen fought against the memory of a sensation: flying above the trees, watching the ground, spying the scurrying shadow of her prey. Folding her wings to drop on top of it. This was the image, the desire that God had given her. It could not be ignored; it had to be reconciled.

"You made my heart the heart of a hunter," she said. "Yet

You forbid senseless killing. What is it that You wish me to hunt, that it is not senseless to kill?"

Do you know, you never actually feel yourself kill, do you? You fold your wings, and drop—you feel the rush of wind, and know success, but that is where the vision ends. You do not see your prey and do not feel its death between your talons. The prey might as well be imaginary. And yet that does not matter to you. What matters is the hunt.

Lhennuen was surprised, and was silent.

One does not necessarily have to hunt with the intention of causing death, God said. What is the hunt, but movement, and seeking? This year, when not at your duties, you have been flying, and walking, and learning—from books, from Tayitoös—which is seeking after knowledge. And you have felt at peace.

"When I am doing one of those things, yes. But they don't make a life."

Because you want your actions to make some improvement in the world.

"That," Lhennuen said, without apology, "is human."

It certainly is.

"And?" Lhennuen said, after a moment. "There's only one house left to build, here...."

And so what improvement do you wish to work toward? God asked patiently.

She did not hesitate. "Peace."

You have all the facts, God said. Now might be a good time to think outside the box.

Lhennuen sat through the night many hours, and thought.

Just before dawn, she rose. Beneath a witchlight, she carried Yugho's body into the ash, laid him down, and kissed him gently.

It took her a long time to come to giving the funeral rites, as she stood over him and wept silently for a departed soul and a lost future. As it turned out, she was human after all. But at last she gave the rites, with only a dance of her hands in place of words as Yugho might have wished. And she set his body on fire.

When the fire was down, and the light was up, she walked deep in thought, following no path. Wondering about what things she would see and learn in her travels in Tsiani lands; as she worked toward peace the slow way, one friend at a time.

But this time, unlike the last, she would make good-byes before she went. To her family, to her friends, to her fellow priests, to people whose lives had touched hers. She would help the people of Herede build their last house, and celebrate its completion with them. And she would probably cry in front of them.

The weight that was on her was the weight of sorrow at leaving friends behind, rather than the weight of having to fulfill social necessity.

"What do you know," she said softly to the cool autumn dawn before taking flight. "Personal growth for Lhennuen Damaiud."

* * *

Where to Find the Author

Web: emepps.com
Blog: blog.emepps.com
Facebook: facebook.com/EMEppsWriter
Twitter: twitter.com/emepps
Goodreads: bit.ly/emeppsgr
Pinterest: pinterest.com/emepps

To receive a **free, exclusive short story by E. M. Epps**, head over to emepps.com/signup and subscribe to the author's newsletter. In addition to the free story, subscribers receive first notice of new stories, plus perks like sneak peeks, discounts, and the chance to enter for giveaways!

Other Works by the Author

THE INTERPRETER'S TALE: A WORD WITH TOO MANY MEANINGS, a novel of languages and diplomacy.

As a linguist and military interpreter, Eliadmaru Faraa has always been a supporting character in other people's stories. And so far, that's been just fine with him: it's words he loves, not swordplay or affairs of state.

Now he's been asked for help by the Emperor's nephew. Together, along with an irritating ambassador and a sorceress with a secret and a high sex drive, they aim to save an ailing princess and stop the trade of weapons to the border war.

Which is more difficult—not disgracing himself during a touchy negotiation, winning back his boyhood sweetheart, or translating his lovelorn teenage boss's amateur poetry?

He'll soon find out....

Hello, Reader! This is your author speaking. I hope you enjoyed this book! I'd like to think you did, since you made it to the last page.

May I ask a small favor of you? Will you take a moment now to rate and review this book on your favorite book site, whether that's Amazon, iTunes, Goodreads or elsewhere? You don't have to get fancy—this isn't English class. You certainly don't need to write a synopsis or a three-page analysis of the themes! But I would deeply appreciate if you'd share just a sentence or two saying what you loved or hated about it.

A single review may seem so insignificant as to be not worth bothering with, but truthfully, EVERY review is hugely important, because reviews are how other readers will decide whether they even want to TRY a book. Your review may be the one that connects with someone and helps them decide.

So, if you like my work, will you please share with the world what you like about it? And if there's something specific about it that you dislike, that's valuable feedback too, both for me as a writer and for other readers!

And if you REALLY like what you've read, please join me by subscribing to my updates list at http://www.emepps.com/signup. That way you'll always be the first to know when I have new books available—AND you'll get a free story just for subscribing!

The Interpreter's Tale is the only fantasy novel ever told from the perspective of a diplomatic interpreter: a role both ubiquitous and vital in the real world, but thoroughly neglected in both realistic and speculative fiction—until now.

"If you've ever wondered what it's like to be a polyglot, *The Interpreter's Tale* will introduce you to a fantastical world of intrigue, trouble and tongue-play. If you are a polyglot, you can commiserate with Eliadmaru constantly being the only one in the room who can understand what everyone else is saying. Extremely fun read!"
—David J. Peterson, creator of the Dothraki language for HBO's *Game of Thrones* and author of *Living Language Dothraki*

THE PORTRAIT OF GÉRALDINE GERMAINE, a novelette of love and art.

It's almost the turn of the century in Paris, and Géraldine Germaine is an independent woman. She rides a bicycle, scoffs at the ridiculous fashions in hats, and makes a living (barely) by writing a melodramatic weekly serial (published under a man's name, of course). She loves her work, and life is beautiful—even if the ceiling of her attic apartment *is* so low she can't sit up in bed.

Then she starts to notice certain coincidences shared between her life and her fictional heroine's. Little things, at first.

But then...she meets a painter who looks just like the hero of her story.

And he wants her to be *his* muse....

"*Il est adorable!* This romantic gem of a novelette will please lovers of *Amélie* and *Chocolat*. As vibrant as a freshly cut rose!"
—Celeste Bradley, *New York Times* bestselling author

TO HELL AND BACK AGAIN...WITH A LITTLE WHITE DOG, a novella of myth and magic.

Geoffrey Keyes has hired magicians Morris and Cathleen Madison to rescue his impetuous stepdaughter Anastasia after her foolhardy trip to Hell goes (rather unsurprisingly) wrong. But there are so many things he doesn't understand. Why has Anastasia gone to Hell at all? What, or who, is holding her there? What has a pomegranate got to do with blood sacrifices?

And most importantly—why do Mr. and Mrs. Madison insist on bringing their little white dog with them into Hell?

Made in the USA
Charleston, SC
29 September 2015